Martha Bacon has drawn on the years she lived in Africa and Europe for the varied backgrounds and characterizations in SOPHIA SCROOBY PRESERVED. She now lives in Rhode Island, and has related the American setting of her story to the African origins of her invincible heroine.

The author is an experienced novelist and poet who teaches, among other subjects, a course on children's literature for teachers. She and her husband, Professor R. B. Ballinger, are both on the faculty at Rhode Island College. She has written for such magazines as the *Atlantic, Saturday Review* and *Vogue*. Martha Bacon skillfully combines her perception of people and places with a love of adventure in SOPHIA SCROOBY PRESERVED, her first book for children.

David Omar White has been inspired by his own children to create several ingenious and popular picture books. His drawings are touched with humor, and Pansy emerges a vivid figure with grace and style. Mr. White studied in California, principally at The Claremont Graduate School, under Henry Lee McFee. He currently does illustrations and satiric drawings.

OPHIA

CROOBY

RESERVED

# SOPHIA SCROOBY PRESERVED

by MARTHA BACON

*Illustrated by David Omar White*

*An Atlantic Monthly Press Book*
BOSTON　Little, Brown and Company　TORONTO

LIBRARY OF CONGRESS CATALOG CARD NO. 68–21167

FIRST EDITION

I am indebted to W. S. Lewis's lecture: "A Tour Through London: 1776" for much of the detail contained in Chapters Sixteen and Seventeen.

M.B.B.

ATLANTIC–LITTLE, BROWN BOOKS
ARE PUBLISHED BY
LITTLE, BROWN AND COMPANY
IN ASSOCIATION WITH
THE ATLANTIC MONTHLY PRESS

*Published simultaneously in Canada*
*by Little, Brown & Company (Canada) Limited*

PRINTED IN THE UNITED STATES OF AMERICA

*This book is for:*

MICHAEL SEBASTIAN QUIMBY

MARTIN GREGORY NELSON &

CHRISTIAN STEVEN ESKELUND

## The Riddle

My first: Pearl
My second: Aurora
My third: Night
My fourth: Sun
My fifth: Youth
My whole: Pansy

SOPHIA

SCROOBY

PRESERVED

# CHAPTER 1

*In which the reader is introduced to the heroine of this narrative and learns of her birth, parentage, early recollections and education in her native land.*

N OR ABOUT the year 1768 a daughter was born to a well-to-do lesser chieftain of an African tribe whose hunting grounds lay somewhat to the north of the Swazi tribes and west of the Tshangans. The chieftain already had a number of sons and so he gave this daughter a somewhat more affectionate welcome than was usually accorded to little girls among his people. He intended to give her a magnificent name when she lost her first baby tooth, the customary time for giving a child a permanent name, but for the time being he called her Nono, meaning Nameless. Nono grew strong and handsome in the great bush country of her birth; she resembled her father who was renowned for his good looks. At four years of age she began to ask questions. Her mother said that she took a great deal of notice for her age and her great-grandmother, old Ani, said that she was spoiled.

Nono noticed that her mother left the family hut early every morning in order to pour water to the sun at his rising.

"Why do you pour water to the sun?" Nono asked her mother.

"Because we have always done it," said her mother. "Why else? When you are older you will do it too. It is one

of the most important duties of the women of this tribe. If we didn't do it the sun might not rise and then where would we be?"

"Have you ever tried *not* doing it to see what would happen?" asked Nono.

"Of course not," said her mother. "That would be breaking a rule. Rules were made to be kept, not broken. Who would wish to break them?"

"Who made the rules?" asked Nono.

"Nobody that I ever heard of," replied her mother with a touch of impatience. "They were here to keep ever since I can remember, and you and I were made to keep them. Bear that in mind and you'll keep out of difficulties."

"But how did we find out what the rules were?" asked Nono.

"The witch doctor tells us. He learned them from his father and his father learned them from *his* father."

"But who told *his* father?" persisted Nono.

"The sun told the pie-crow and the pie-crow told him."

"But why did the pie-crow choose the witch doctor's grandfather? Why not somebody else?"

"Did you ever see such a child for questions?" exclaimed Nono's mother, quite exasperated. "Questions bring bad luck. Girls aren't meant to know the reasons for things. If they did who knows what they would be up to! They would neglect their duties, the village would go to rack and ruin, the sun wouldn't rise and we should probably have to shift ground. You stick to the rules. It's the only way. And besides that's what you were put on earth to do."

"Ooooooh," said Nono, making a sound like wind through the long bushgrass. She was tired of a conversation which seemed to lead only to a lesson in obedience. She left the round, dark, smoky hut and wandered through the compound and out to the edge of the long grass. It was quite early in the morning. Spring had come and the grass was pale green, cool, and not yet very high. Here and there a thornbush struck a zigzag shape, like a show of lightning against the sky. In the distance a fierce row of crags ranged beneath a heavy fleece of cloud.

"Young daughter," called Nono's mother from inside the hut. "If you want breakfast you must milk the goat."

Nono went off to find the nanny goat. She was grazing with all the other goats of the village near the stream below the rampart of dried thorn which walled the little town.

The village was a busy place, and as Nono knew to her regret, hardly anyone had time for her questions. Everyone, or nearly everyone, worked. The men's work was principally hunting and the women tilled the crops, cured the hides brought home by their husbands, drew water and made clay and thatch for the huts.

Among the idle of the village — mainly babies — was the witch doctor, although he claimed to work harder than anyone else. Nono would have liked to ask a great many questions about his work. It consisted chiefly of painting his face, and dancing. He danced when the corn needed rain and when the men went hunting. He danced when someone got married and he danced for hours on end at seed time and at harvest time. If the rains came and the buck were plentiful and the married couple didn't quarrel and the corn came up the witch doctor reminded the village that it was all because of his dancing.

But if the weather stayed dry and the game hid itself and the bride returned to her father's hut asking for her bride-price back and the corn burned on the stalk, the witch doctor went on dancing until things changed. If someone was stepped on by an elephant or someone refused to pay a debt of cows and goats to someone else, the witch doctor danced until the elephant quieted down and the creditors were satisfied. Whenever a good thing happened the witch doctor said it was all because of his dancing. Whenever things went wrong it was somebody else's fault. He was good enough to put matters right by dancing even faster and more furiously than before. He was always glad to do it, he said. He lived for others and never thought of himself. But it was scandalous how ungrateful people

6

were. Nobody really appreciated how hard he worked for his village. It was all taken for granted. Sometimes he felt ready to leave this thankless place and find a home with a tribe who would know how to value him. Take the matter of food. You would have thought that someone would have seen fit to bring him the more tender portions of the game which he had been at such pains to dance for, rather than the tough stringy bits which his teeth could not manage. But what could you expect of human nature! It was the same the world over, no doubt.

Nono, when she heard this complaint, asked one of her brothers if there was any truth in the statement that human nature was the same the world over, and how large was the world?

"Enormous," said her brother. "We live in the middle of it." And he shifted his spear to his shoulder and joined a group of young braves who were going out after water-buck. Nono was left to entertain herself with the herdboy, the only person in the village who had time for her questions. His answers made very little sense but he enjoyed inventing them. He lay by the stream all day, minding the goats and a few thin cattle, kicking his legs in the air and dozing in the sun. Nono would come and squat beside him and talk. But sometimes she grew tired of conversation with the herdboy, who was incredibly lazy and vain, and would try to trap someone else in her dialogue. She went to her great-grandmother, old Ani, the oldest person in the village. Ani was so old that she could recall the days when the village lay in another part of the bush, a moon's march nearer the sunrise.

Ani was a useful and thoroughly unpleasant old woman

who sat all day in the middle of the village minding a cooking pot and scolding and muttering to herself. When children came teasing her for a bite from the pot she spat and threw sticks at them. She was not only Nono's great-grandmother but nearly everyone else's too.

"Ani," asked Nono, "are there any people in he world besides us?"

"Eh?" cried Ani.

Nono put her hands into the shape of a cup around her mouth and bawled her question into Ani's ear.

"Other people!" squeaked Ani. "Did you say other people?" She spat furiously across the cooking pot into the coals, which hissed angrily. "What a thing to ask! Yes, there used to be some other people. They came down from the north, tramp, tramp, tramp. That was when we were in the other village. Our people killed them all, of course. They should have stayed up north." And she gave Nono a cuff that knocked her down for asking such a preposterous question.

Nono picked herself up and dusted herself off. She did not mind being knocked down by old Ani. Ani made everyone who came within reach bite the dust.

"What did they look like?" she asked.

"Ugly as baboons," said Ani. "They weren't even fit to eat. We gave them to the hyenas. There aren't any more of them. Now get along before I put you in the pot."

Nono, having had enough of old Ani, went off in search of someone else and found her father, sitting just outside the village near the stream, sharpening the point of his spear on a stone. He had cast off his mantle of leopard

8

skins and his fine, long limbs gleamed in the sunlight like the hide of the sable antelope. Nono thought him unquestionably the finest warrior in the village and would have been happy to spend all her days in his company. He in turn was proud of her cleverness — all his family were clever, he said, but his little panther was the cleverest of all.

Nono's father lifted his spear and pointed it across the stream.

"Do you see what I see?" he said.

"I see a shadow on the rock," said Nono.

"That shadow has terrible teeth," said her father. As he spoke the shadow yawned. When a crocodile yawns it stays motionless with jaws agape for minutes together.

"You are old enough to learn never to trust a shadow," said Nono's father. "Shadows are dangerous and may have long teeth. If it is in the trees above you it may have a spotted pelt and terrible claws. And if you see no shadow always remember to listen to what the birds are saying.

"What do the birds say?" asked Nono.

"They tell you where the snake runs," said the chieftain. "They speak loudest for the mamba snake."

"Father," said Nono, "are there are any other people in the world?"

"What makes you ask that?" asked her father.

"I asked Ani and she said that there were some but they weren't fit to eat. Then she said she would put me in the pot if I asked any more questions."

"Ani has been pretending to put people in the pot ever since I was no higher than you," said Nono's father.

"However, you *do* ask too many questions. Altogether too many."

"If you will only tell me about the other people I shall ask no more questions."

"That is a vain promise," said the chieftain. "One question leads to another and the day ends in nothing but talk. If I tell you about the people, you will be wanting to know what they wore and what they ate and whether they were like us or different."

"What *were* they like?" asked Nono.

"Like us," replied her father. "They came down from the north with long knives. We fought a battle and many of us were killed. Others were taken prisoner and marched with the enemy to the southwest. We never saw the prisoners again nor learned what befell them. And once a stranger came from the south. He came all alone and rode a creature like a zebra but without stripes. He was white as the moon and so was his creature. It obeyed all his commands. I did not see him but my mother's brother did. He came among my mother's brother's people when I was not so tall as the grass is now. He told strange and terrible things. My mother's brother's people had more than half a mind to kill this moon-man, but they did not in the end lest they offend his gods. It was clear that he was very powerful. He cast a darkness over the sky at midday. He ordered the sun to hide itself and it obeyed just as his creature obeyed. Presently he went away to the south again. The people were very much afraid."

Nono shivered. The thought of a man as white as the moon horrified her. What a ghastly spectacle he must have been! She left her father testing his spear and went back to the village. Old Ani was still sitting over the pot, hissing evil things at it.

"Times have certainly changed," said old Ani. "Things aren't what they used to be. The children are badly brought up, not what they were in my day at all. No manners. And I never saw such a useless lot of goats as this village keeps nowadays. And there's no feeding off the game our men catch now. It wouldn't satisfy a jackal. And the girls are the worst of the lot. Not one of them will do an honest day's work. Just sit about and gossip all day long." She saw Nono and gave a cackle. "And you're the worst of the lot. You do nothing but ask questions. Not the faintest use in the world and never will be. Your parents spoil you."

Nono ran around Ani in a wide circle and went outside the village where the wind was parting the grass and where lately an elephant had been. Nono knew this from the newly trampled grass where he had walked and the thorn-bush which he had uprooted and thrown aside. She walked a little way and presently she came upon the herdboy, sitting on a stone, playing his kalimba. He held the little harplike instrument in his hands and pressed the music from the reeds with his two thumbs. The music came faint on the breeze as though from very far away. Nono loved it and paused for a moment to listen before beginning to talk.

"Did you know that we aren't the only people?" she said presently. "My father says so. One of them is white as the moon."

"More people!" said the herdboy. "Don't be silly. What would they eat? Why there's barely enough for us. And where would they live? You can see for yourself that there are no people. I don't suppose they live in the sky, or in the water like frogs."

"Perhaps there are other villages a long way off where we can't see them," said Nono.

"But you can see the sky all around you," said the herdboy, "and there are no villages. It's quite impossible."

"I should like to be sure of it," said Nono.

"Well, you can't be," said the herdboy. He was getting bored and hungry. "Nobody can be certain about some things. And even if they could it would be no business of yours. Your job is to plant corn and tend babies and mend thatch. And you must learn to cook. If you learn to cook and also grow up to be very good-looking with a lovely disposition I might marry you. I don't promise anything but I might. Then you would have no time for asking questions. You would be too busy seeing that you were worth your bride-price to ask about other people. Besides, there aren't any and if there were our people would have killed them all in a great victory."

"Even the moon-man?"

"Him first of all," said the herdboy.

"And his creature?"

"What creature?"

"The zebra without stripes."

"Who cares for a zebra without stripes? They would eat it. I would eat it now if I could. I should eat it all and let you have the tail if you liked."

Nono rather hoped that the herdboy wouldn't be so good as to marry her when she grew up. And she had no wish to eat the moon-man's creature, although she was eager to see it. A zebra without stripes must be a great curiosity, she thought. She stared across the plain where she could see a herd of red impala grazing in a clump of thornbushes. The bucks had beautifully curved horns like the frame of a kalimba. If they would grow reeds between their horns they would make magnificent music. She could almost imagine the wind sweeping the music between their antlers. The impala moved together in a group, save for the sentries who stood apart keeping watch for lion. There were a few zebra grazing among them because the zebra and the impala are friends. At a greater distance Nono saw something black moving against the sky. It was probably an elephant. As the afternoon wore on she lazily observed quite a number of commonplace animals. She saw three giraffe glide like great golden ghosts through the long grass, followed by a herd of wildebeest. They looked fierce with their sharp horns and curly moustaches but when Nono tossed a stone in their direction the whole herd ran off in a panic. She saw a baboon who climbed a thornbush and spat at her. Nono spat back. She hated baboons. She saw a gray monkey who came and begged so passionately for some of the herdboy's food that it actually got a morsel or two. It was more than Nono could have done. On the whole it was just a dull African afternoon. Nothing ever happens here, thought Nono. It was always just the same. A few elephant, a few giraffe, a zebra or two and the bush stretching away in all directions forever. The

1 3

thornbushes melted into the shadows; the shadows shifted into other shadows and the day slid into twilight as a snake slides under a leaf.

It was more amusing at twilight because the lion came to the water hole and roared. The hippopotamus gave an answering roar, and wallowed and churned up the mud. When the stars began to glow like a cheetah's eyes, the herdboy played a little lullaby on his kalimba and drove the goats back to the village. Old Ani gave Nono and the herdboy their supper and scolded them for being so late.

"Serve you right if the lions ate you," she said. "Two less mouths to feed and not so many questions to answer."

Nono and the herdboy ate as much as old Ani would give them, which was not nearly as much as they would have liked, and then each one went to his own hut. They slept as usual. The night birds whistled and cried. Out in the bush the hyena laughed. But if Nono had listened she would have heard the sound of feet — tramp, tramp, tramp. Other people were coming down from the north.

# CHAPTER 2

*In which Nono the Nameless begins a long journey and makes the acquaintance of beasts and men of all sorts and conditions.*

NONO WOKE UP in the darkness. At first she thought her mother was pounding corn but as she came awake she realized that the pounding noise came from beyond the hut. It was loud and growing louder. The earth was shaking under giant footsteps. She opened her mouth to speak but before the words left her lips she saw her father leap from his mat, catch up the spear which he had been sharpening by the river yesterday afternoon, and dash out of the hut. Then came a sound which Nono had been told about but had never heard with her own ears. It was the war cry of her tribe. The yell seemed to tear Nono off her mat and pitch her into the middle of the village. The village was on fire. Every thatch was ablaze and every man, woman and child was running away from something or toward something — it was impossible to tell which. Through smoke and flame Nono could see the dark glint of the long knives and hear the terrified screaming of the word "Zulu! Zulu!" Spears flew through the flames and people fell down and vanished in the smoke. Trapped in their pen the goats were bleating pitifully. Nono ran to the pen and threw open the gate and the goats streamed out, galloping helter-skelter for the river with Nono after them. She had some confused thought that everyone would be glad to see the goats when the battle was over.

Nono could see neither of her parents, nor the herdboy nor old Ani nor any of her brothers nor the witch doctor. People rushed past her through the burning village but they were all strangers. By the time she reached the river she was alone except for the goats. The sky was red over the village and the noise of the battle persisted but here by the river all was quiet. The moon shone down on the scaly back of the crocodile as he floated downstream. Along the opposite bank the fever trees stood in a pale green row and no wind ruffled their leaves.

Nono could not have told how long she crouched among the goats by the river. The sun came up and the red glow in the sky died away. The bush, the plain, the sky were as silent and motionless as a rock-painting. Nono herself sat like a rock-painting, watching the sickly shimmering trees on the bank across the river and waiting for something to break the stillness. A giraffe moved softly through the grove of fever trees, his head high among the topmost branches, like some tall, tawny lily. He splayed his knees, bent his long neck and drank from the river, then went away as softly and slowly as he had come, moving as though carried by the wind. Then a lioness came with three cubs and drank. They paid no attention to Nono, squatting on the bank. Perhaps she dreamed them. Or perhaps she was nothing but a dream herself — a dream who was dreaming it was a child. But even a dream can dream of hunger so Nono finally milked the nanny goat and had breakfast. Then she walked a short distance up the riverbank until she came to a crab apple tree where she ate a green crab apple. While she was eating the crab apple she looked across the plain to where the village had been and saw a group of people — a column of armed men marching against the sky. Even at that distance she could see that they were not her people. Her tribe had never marched so. And the helmets were of a different shape from those worn by her father and brothers. These people carried shields of a kind Nono had never seen. Some were red, some were black and white, others brown and yellow. The column marched in a stiff, orderly fashion. Once there was a sharp cry and the whole column came to a halt, locked shields, made a clashing sound with its spears and then, as though it were all one long snakelike body, turned and marched to the southwest, tramp, tramp, tramp. Nono stood watching them. Now she had seen the other people — the all-conquering Zulu, the deadly sons of the Matabele, marching down from the north.

But what of the village? Was there nobody left? Gathering her courage, Nono turned from the river and started toward her home.

The bush was hideously silent. Save for the goats she was the only living creature in sight. She looked upward and her heart sprang up, a fountain of fear in her breast. The sky was full of vultures. And before her stood a dark smouldering pile of burned thatch and fire-blackened clay. Not a sound came from it and over it hung the vultures, circling lower and lower in the blinding sunlight.

Nono turned from the burned village in bewilderment. Somewhere to the southwest the Zulu were marching on their terrible journey. Whatever she did she must not risk an encounter with them. The only thing to do was to march in the opposite direction. So Nono marched north-east.

It was a long march. Nono walked — step after step — until she thought that any moment the bush must come to an end and she would find herself walking in the sky. This did not happen. The sky remained where it was and Nono walked through groves of thornbush, through waving parklands of grass, through dry ditches where she went warily for fear of wild dog, through small forests of fever trees — and still the bush went on, always changing, always the same: the great African bush which is forever moving and forever still. Sometimes a sweet, strong smell came to Nono on the wind and she knew that lion was nearby. Sometimes she could smell elephant. Toward evening she came upon a dead buck, hanging in a thornbush, and she knew that a leopard had stocked his larder. Nono crept on swiftly, having no wish to interrupt the leopard, and came presently to two impala sentries. She crouched down near them and went to sleep. She slept beside the sentries until morning and when they moved on with the herd Nono moved with them. The impala were moving eastward, grazing as they went, and Nono decided it was wise to remain with them. The small bucks with their long curved horns looked stately and brave. The does had kind faces and the fauns were gentle and not afraid of Nono. They appeared to think that she was one of them. So Nono stayed with the red impala, drinking where they drank and eating where they ate. She found plenty of crab apples and ate what the elephant left. The elephant loved crab apples and they made it easy for Nono to find the trees by leaving their great crazy tracks to guide her to the orchards. The crab apples made the elephant drunk. They staggered about, trumpeting and boasting after they had gorged themselves on the fruit, and Nono was able to find crab apples nearly every day.

On the whole Nono enjoyed her life with the impala very much. She singled out a particular doe for her foster-mother and slept at night close to her flank with the doe's own faun. By day she played with the fauns, never straying outside the circle. Once when the herd was scared by a cheetah it stampeded, and Nono stampeded with it. She leaped on the back of a half-grown buck who was too terrified to notice that he had a rider. Nono had a very fast and frightening run which lasted so long that she thought she really must have found the end of the bush at last. But when the impala came panting to rest she found herself still among thorns and shadows, among the same patches of sunlight and lacework of leaves as before. The giraffe moved through the fever trees, slim, slow and golden. The elephant rolled over the land or wallowed in the rivers, the buffalo, the zebra, the wildebeest grazed, their young trotting along with the herds. Once in a while Nono met ostrich and when this happened she stole an egg if she could. An ostrich egg kept her going for days.

Nono spent such a long time with the impala that she began to think she was quite a different person from the one she had been when she walked away from the burned village and the Zulu Impi. Instead of being round and plump she was long and thin. She thought of herself as a bush-shadow and sometimes she thought of herself as an impala.

But one day the bush really did come to an end. The

ground began to rise and Nono found herself climbing. She had reached the foot of a mountain. She had come such a distance by now that she thought it would be silly to stop for a mere mountain. She would go to the top, if only to see what was there. The impala wouldn't come. The bucks locked horns and began to play games. The does stood by watching to see which of the young princes would disentangle himself first. When one buck would decide that he was beaten another buck would take his place. The buck who succeeded in never lifting his head was the winner and had his pick of the does. There was no place for Nono in this game. She stole away from the impala and started to make her way up the mountain. She was after all a stranger to the tribe of antelope and could never really play their games.

Nono climbed all morning. Halfway up the mountain the underbrush disappeared and the ground became bare and stony. Once a lizard, half as long as Nono, wriggled out from under a rock and hissed at her, giving her a horrible fright. Overhead a buzzard circled, watching and waiting for a kill. Toward evening, Nono came to the top of the mountain — and from this place she could see the whole world. It was so large that its size took her breath away. She perceived that it was round as the moon but a great deal bigger and more various. Directly below her the world was green and beautiful and a river ran at the foot of the mountain among green trees. It looked like a lovely place. If she hurried she fancied she might come to that charming grove before nightfall. She made as much haste as possible — it is always quicker to go down a mountain than up — and Nono's descent was fairly rapid. She found herself at midafternoon in a forest. Here the trees were taller than any tree she had seen in the bush. Great garlands hung from their branches and the ground was strewn with pink and white star-shaped flowers. Kingfishers flashed through the trees. There were bluebirds, yellow orioles, birds with scarlet feathers, and a great black bird with a white hood who looked at Nono with hard, yellow eyes. The air in the forest was warm and damp and as the trees thinned out it became warmer and damper. She came presently to a cluster of trees that did not resemble anything she had ever seen before. They had leaves as large as the shields carried by the Zulu warriors and each tree bore a clump of yellow fruit. Nono knew fruit when she saw it. She shied a stone at a clump and brought down several bananas. She ate them with relish and when she had finished she curled up under one of the trees and went to sleep in the shade of the great green fronds.

Nono slept from sunset until dawn under the banana tree and when morning came, having feasted on several more bananas, she continued her walk. She reached the end of the banana plantation and saw a group of dwellings. Although they in no way resembled the round thatched huts of her childhood she could see that this honeycomb of a place was a village and not to be confused with anything else. These houses were for the most part white and square, the ground beneath her feet was rough with stones and there were people everywhere. And what people — not one tribe but hundreds of tribes. To sort them out was impossible. There were people of every color, some dark, like Nono, some of a medium shade of brown, dressed in long white robes which floated about them like clouds, and some of the people were clearly relatives of the moon-man who had visited her father's mother's brother's people. Their clothes fitted their bodies closely and the general effect was awkward and uncomfortable. Nono was surprised that the people were all of plain colors. None were striped like zebra or spotted like leopard. There were also in this village animals whose like she had never seen, and they bore only the remotest resemblance to the creatures of the bush. She saw dogs, cats, pigs and chickens. She saw a donkey who laid back his ears and made a sound as shocking as the laugh of a hyena. She saw the moon-men riding their unstriped zebra. She had assumed from what her father had said that the moon-man was the only one of his kind but here she was undeceived. The moon-men were numerous and also quite powerful. She thought they must have come originally from the moon because of their pale skins and she wondered how they made the journey. It must have been a terrible trip.

The village was altogether an alarming place, noisy, full of bad smells and incomprehensible sights and possible dangers. The dogs barked at her and frightened her badly but the people all seemed much too busy to take any notice of her. During that day of wandering about the town Nono began to feel that she did not exist at all. But as usual poor Nono was hungry and for all her wandering she could find nothing that suggested itself to her as food. She wondered how everyone else managed. There were other young children like herself wandering about but nobody seemed inclined to feed them. In her village there had always been old Ani and her pot and there was food in the bush for those who looked for it but here in this crowded lair of men there was nothing to eat — not an ostrich egg, nor a handful of crab apples — not even a frog.

Nono was appalled by all the strangeness. She saw carts with wheels, which puzzled her dreadfully. She saw people working with tools, and the tools were not of stone or wood or the horns of animals but of another material, something hard and shining which gave a queer ringing cry when it struck another object. The sound frightened Nono. It was both loud and lifeless as though the dead had cried out. She walked down alley after alley, trying somehow to escape the cry of the metal, but wherever she went it followed her.

The sun was bright and the sky was a sheet of searing blue and finally when Nono thought that the streets would never stop winding into other hot, white-walled dusty streets she came out into a clearing. She found herself standing on a strip of sand and beyond the sand lay the end of the world.

Only a short running distance lay between Nono and the great sky lapping at the edge of the world. It was darker blue than the sky above it, this sky which lay below the land — but still she thought it must be sky because it was full of white clouds moving restlessly across it. Nono ran to meet the sky and felt it running cold over her hot, dusty feet. It was wet like water. But when Nono bent down to taste it she knew that here was no river. For the taste of this fallen sky was the taste of tears and it was not good to drink.

# CHAPTER 3

*In which Nono takes her leave of the Stone Age south of the Sahara and is made acquainted with modern methods of sea travel.*

ITH THE TASTE of tears salting her mouth Nono turned back disconsolate toward the town. The air was cooler now and a salt breeze was blowing. Palm trees tossed gray-green heads above the flat roofs of the town and the sky above and the sky below were full of clouds. West of the town the sun was setting and a few lights began to glow behind the narrow slits of windows in the white-walled houses. Wreaths of smoke began to rise. Nono could smell food cooking. They were unfamiliar odors which came to her nostrils but she was sure that they were those of food. She was so hungry that she began to whine and whimper like a cub in the bush. She began her wanderings all over again, stumbling aimlessly down one darkening street after another, and came presently to a square. In the middle of the square there was a small round structure with some women clustered about it and when Nono drew near she heard the soft splashing of water. The women were drawing water from a well and gossiping among themselves. Nono managed to creep up to the well to catch a few drops of water in her hands as the pails spilled over on the cobblestones.

On one side of the square there was a long, low building, half roofed over and half open to the sky. People were lounging in and out of this place or squatting on its steps, eating and drinking. Drawn by the scent of the food, Nono approached the building, somewhat apprehensively. The place wore a barren, threatening aspect. The people there were all of her color. They were wearing garlands of that same heavy cold material which she had seen put to so many uses around the town that day. The garlands did not strike her as a very pleasant or practical adornment, especially as they were worn by several people at once. Four or five men were attached to each other in such a way that if one man moved all his closest friends had to move too. This was certainly a most interesting tribal custom and one which Nono could not have imagined. Curiosity overcame fear and Nono crept closer and closer in order to examine the strange sight. Only men wore the garlands. This came as no surprise to Nono since in her tribe the men enjoyed many privileges not allowed to the women. But in this case the women clearly had the best of things since they could move about freely. The children also ran free. Nono tried a greeting in her own language. The words came in a halting stutter. It was so long since Nono had spoken to anyone that she had all but forgotten what words were for. She had chattered and sung little tunes to the impala fauns but they were indifferent to words and to music and she had soon joined them in their peaceable silence, putting speech from her mind.

Now these people received her words in silence. They glanced at her as though they did not care whether she lived or died and after a gloomy look or two simply glared into space. So Nono sat down and watched them. Presently a moon-man appeared with a sack of meal and whistled. From holes and corners a great many women and children appeared and fell to their knees holding out their hands. The moon-man poured a measure of meal into each pair of outstretched hands and when he came to Nono he poured meal into her hands too, without giving her a second glance. Nono ate thankfully. She had never suffered so badly from hunger in her life.

Presently the moon-man came and herded everyone, Nono included, into a shed and shut the door. There in the thick reeking darkness Nono fell into a heavy sleep. And this was how Nono the Nameless came to be sold with fifty other persons to a Portuguese slave trader in the port of Moçambique on the southeast coast of Africa.

He came to fetch all his people one morning about a week after Nono's arrival at the great hut which she learned was known as a barracoon. He drove his prisoners down the narrow streets to the place where the sky washed the world. There they were shoved protesting into a boat. Nono had no notion of what a boat was and was hideously frightened. She could only suppose along with all the others that it was some sort of instrument which would remove her to the moon or even possibly beyond it and she wept bitterly at the thought of leaving the world. The tears streamed down her cheeks and the water surged around the boat and splashed her face and she wondered how many people had cried to make that terrible, cold, salty sky. She poured more water to the sun at his rising on that day than her mother had poured during her entire life.

The boat took its unhappy passengers out to the middle

of the bay and then they were pushed and prodded up a perilously swinging ladder, loaded onto a ship, and flung into a dark enclosure. There were shouts and creakings and slammings and finally the quiet of complete despair as the captives gave up all hope. The ship rocked and pitched, the prisoners crouched together in the darkness, sighing and moaning, and nearly all of them wished themselves dead.

Nono and her fellow prisoners made a sea voyage of several weeks. First they sailed southwest and rounded the Cape of Good Hope. The sea was rough and they were all seasick. The waves washed the decks, the sun shot through clouds and the Portuguese sailors climbed the masts to draw in the sails.

"Adamastor, Adamastor," cried the sailors as a pale point of land came into view. Two great purple clouds like ostrich feathers drifted across the face of the sun. Other clouds formed themselves into wings over the sky. Nono, who had been brought up on deck with others of the women and children, forgot to be miserable. The fresh wind fanned her cheek, a light rain pricked her shoulders and the sun mingled with the rain to throw a warmth upon her. A rainbow leaped over the flat-topped mountain that rose in the distance.

"Adamastor!" cried the sailors, "Lord of the Cape!"

On the whole, life on this ship was not too bad for Nono, once she got used to it. The ship had a name. It was called the *Isabella de Castro*. It was new and the captain took great pride in it. The prisoners were only a part of the cargo. They had been put aboard the *Isabella de Castro* to make weight because there was a shortage of the sugarcane which the captain had expected to take on at Moçambique. So the prisoners shared the hold with a pile of leopard skins, some elephant tusks, several bales of spices from Zanzibar — Nono did not know where Zanzibar was — and a cage of baboons who were being brought to someone who lived on the other side of Africa. He never received them because the baboons caught cold and died. The Portuguese sailors were all moon-men. Nono thought at first that they would be different from other people in some important way but in this she was wrong. Except for their skins they were exactly like everyone else. They were in fact remarkably ordinary men. They talked and quarreled among themselves. A number of them were lazy and hoped that anyone but themselves would perform their tasks. They were nothing more than human beings of the usual kind.

Nono picked up a few words of the Portuguese language, just enough to beg for food. The sailors thought this extremely funny and encouraged her with tidbits from their own plates. In this way she was able to vary and increase her diet. She was always careful to divide whatever delicacy she had got hold of with her nearest neighbors as she had been taught to do in the village.

The men prisoners were put to work about the ship. The women and children passed their time telling stories and waiting to see what would happen next. Nono picked up a little of their language too. They were all of one tribe which had been raided by Arabs — Arabs it seemed were the brown men in cloud cloaks whom she had observed on her walk through Moçambique — and sold to the trader. They were all slaves, one woman explained to her, though nobody knew to what use they would be put. A rumor that they were all to be eaten persisted although when or by whom nobody dared guess.

Finally the ship made a landing and not on the moon either. It docked at a great port of the Gold Coast, a city too huge to be real, or so Nono thought, and too ugly not to be. It reminded Nono of the huge crawling anthills of the bush. There was a chief in this city named Kwame, a man of vast powers. Everyone, black and white, feared him. Rumor ran about the ship that he was master of the sun and could blot it out if he wished or send it bowling down the sky as men send cattle to a pen. Nono actually got a sight of him when she was taken from the *Isabella de Castro* with the others to be inspected. He showed great disappointment in Nono and her friends. He moved among them in his long red and yellow robes, pointing and shouting, thrusting out his heavy underlip and spitting like a baboon. From the faces he made it was clear that he did not intend to eat anyone. The people he ate, he seemed to say, were of a better quality than these. He stalked off in a rage at last and the captain of the *Isabella de Castro* screamed after him like a leopard. After this Nono and the others were marched into a barracoon and left there.

There were people all over the place: white people, black people, brown people and yellow people with strange narrow eyes. Nono, crouching in the shadow of the barracoon, listened and waited. She tried hard to find out what they were all saying. Once in a while she caught a bit of Portuguese but these people talked Guinean, Arabic, Hindi, Chinese, English and French besides many African dialects. It was like the jabber of monkeys. There was constant quarreling over the exchange of something called money which, as one of the women prisoners explained to Nono, was of great value. The woman could not tell Nono why it was so powerful but the possessor of even a little of it was sure of the envy of others. Nono began to speculate on the possibility of getting her hands on some money. Nothing practical occurred to her, however, and it seemed likely that she would probably have to manage, as she had in the past, without money. She wondered if money was some kind of spirit and if it would be worthwhile to pray to it — or, as the witch doctor might have done, dance for it. These thoughts were idle ones for Nono did neither, but merely moped through the hours with the other prisoners.

Then one day when Nono had begun to think that perhaps she would remain in the barracoon forever she and all the others were driven to the square where their Portuguese owner exchanged them all for money. Everyone was selling somebody else that day. There were white men selling black men and black men selling other black men. There were white men selling chiefs and one chief who sold only white men. And finally somebody bought Nono. He bought a great many other people too, most of Nono's companions on the *Isabella de Castro* and others who were brought weeping and fighting from other parts of the continent. For some hours the sale resembled a battle. People refused to be sold. Knives flashed in the air and there were sharp thunderous explosions which felled a number of people before the day was out.

It was almost a relief to the child at the end of this

ferocious day to find herself on a ship again. She knew a ship for what it was by now. She also knew that the cold garlands worn by the prisoners were iron chains. And she knew the difference between the sea and the sky.

Not that it made much difference to her in the end. On this ship she rarely saw either one. She lived in a steaming darkness, only just aware that she existed, remembering nothing, hoping for nothing. The waters of the Middle Passage, the stormy route of the slavers to the New World, closed over the bodies of many of her companions, and if she had been able to understand what she felt when this happened, as it did with dreadful frequency, she might have said that the most sorrowful aspect of these deaths was that death had ceased to have meaning for all these people. It had no meaning for Nono, yet she continued to live. She lived and she lost one of her front teeth.

The voyage seemed to be without a purpose and without a destination. The ship sailed always toward the sunset; some of the prisoners thought it might be going to the moon. But since the moon never seemed to get nearer but behaved in the usual way, looking sometimes no more than a sliver of melon rind and at other times like the whole melon, few people put much faith in this idea.

The only thing that changed on the voyage was the weather. It got worse. The slaver *Salvation* shivered and groaned as the waves punished her. In spite of the horrible crowding the slave quarters grew cold. The prisoners fell ill and died by the score while the ship struggled forward with the survivors, sailing westward to the end of the world.

Every now and then the women and children were taken from the hold and brought up on deck for an hour or two.

Then Nono learned that some of the white men who sailed the ship were as wretched as the prisoners. They cringed about the vessel doing their tasks, wincing like jackals at the shouts of the captain and the mates. There were frequent floggings. One day a man was hanged from the crosspiece of the highest mast until he was dead, while the women and children crouched on the deck, watching his swinging body with dull eyes.

And when the prisoners were fed their scant and barely palatable rations some of these sailors watched them in a way that made Nono pity the poor creatures as much as she pitied herself and her fellow prisoners. They reminded her of hyenas waiting for the last of the kill, their brown eyes brimful of tears of hunger.

Nono was crouching by the rail one day, eating a piece of bread which she had saved over from the last ration. While she was gnawing it slowly — it was terribly leathery — she saw one of the white men watching her. Something about his look aroused Nono to a kind of longing. His sorrowful eyes yearned at the bread as at a lion's kill. Nono tore off half her piece of bread and thrust the morsel into the man's hands.

The man looked at the bread as though it were a miracle and as though now that he had it he could not imagine what to do with it. Then he snapped it as a hyena snaps a bone. He ate it in two swallows and gave Nono another look — he made a queer wry face — he was trying to smile. Then he spoke.

"God bless you, Pansy-eyes," he said. The words meant nothing to Nono but she turned her large eyes on the man and smiled in reply.

Nono did not see the man again for a long time although she looked for him whenever she was brought up for air. These trips were infrequent for the weather was cold and grew colder as the days passed. There was almost no sight of the sun. But one day when Nono was shivering in the spray and watching the sea wrinkling below the ship, dark gray like the hide of a rhinoceros, she saw her sailor again. He looked even more like a jackal than ever with his starved body and begging eyes. Nono had no bread to give him but he had something for her. It was a length torn from a tattered sail. The sailor had cut a hole in the middle of it. He slipped the garment over Nono's head and it covered her to the knees.

"Keep that, Pansy-eyes; it'll keep you warm. Remember me. You did me a good turn and I'll not forget it. If we meet again in happier times we'll be friends." It was because of this sailor that Nono came to be listed on the bill of lading from the *Salvation* as "one wench, Pansy."

And that was the last that Nono ever saw of him. A few days, or perhaps hours, later — she had lost track of time on this voyage — amid noise and confusion the journey came to an end. Nono, with the other survivors of this ordeal, was taken ashore, marched into another barracoon and left in the cold and darkness to wonder what would come next.

The ship had been unloaded in the evening and the evening was followed in due course by a morning. It was a pale, cold morning at first but it brightened into full daylight presently and the sun shone through the bars of the barracoon.

Nono was wretched with cold and hunger but her fright had somewhat subsided. She no longer expected to be eaten. Nobody would want to eat such a skeleton as herself. Indeed it was a puzzle to decide what anyone would want with her. Nono remembered how strong and sleek she had been in the days when she ran with the impala herd. Lion hunted her in those days and were proud to do it, she thought. Now she wasn't fit feeding for a vulture.

Day followed day in this new barracoon — cold days in which there was nothing to do but shiver. The prisoners sighed and groaned in their shed and longed only for the end of the world. From time to time people came to inspect them. Most of these people were white but once a black man came. He was a huge, strong fellow, somewhat resembling the Kwame of the Gold Coast. The prisoners whispered that he came as a deliverer, being one of their own kind, but they soon learned differently. He bought two of the healthiest of the men and drove them off, chained, with a whip cracking across their backs. He was indeed like the Kwame.

One morning, perhaps a week after her arrival, although it seemed longer, Nono was awakened by a particularly bright shaft of sunlight through the bars. She rose from her corner and went to the window to find out why the sunlight was so piercing. And when she looked out of the window she gave a shout. Some spell had fallen over this strange land. It had vanished under a mantle of glittering white. Even the leafless bush which grew in a corner of the yard had broken into white bloom. For a moment Nono forgot her miseries at the sight of the new-fallen snow. She stared out the window and because she was without words she burst out laughing. She laughed uproariously and while she was still shaking with wild laughter she felt suddenly that she was being watched. She turned from the window and saw a white woman standing in the middle of the room. Nono had seen only white men in her life but this person was unmistakably a woman and a magnificent one at that — a chieftainess perhaps, tall and pale, feathered and furred, wearing a sky-blue cloak that swept the floor, her hands hidden in the white pelt of some animal. There was another woman with her, a black woman, also very finely dressed in a dark cloak and a scarlet turban. Nono stared at these marvels and then dropped her eyes. These people were graceful as impala and when they moved they cast a fragrance about them. They moved slowly, in the manner of creatures who have nothing to dread from life.

The man in charge of the barracoon came in and they

talked with him. He bowed continuously during the conversation and showed a most respectful face to everything said to him. Nono stood before them, looking at the ground and holding her sailcloth dress about her. After a while the white woman opened a fine embroidered purse which hung from her belt and gave the man some money — three silver coins. The man counted the money, gave the woman a little fragment of some thin material with black marks on it, and bowed again. Then one of the women — the black one — took Nono's hand and led her out into the cold, white world.

# CHAPTER 4

*In which Nono the Nameless acquires a name, is introduced to the benefits of learning and the beauties of religion, and becomes a member of polite society.*

ONO'S NEXT SET of experiences were of so confused and bewildering a nature that she was never in afterlife to give a very clear account of them; although she learned later that what befell her was nothing much out of the ordinary. In Africa events had moved slowly, like the rising up and going down of the sun. In the New World they moved with breathtaking speed. What actually occurred within minutes of the exchange of silver for Nono's person was that Nono, wrapped in a blanket, was placed in a carriage between her new mistress and the lady's maid and the carriage set off at a tremendous clip behind a smart coachman and a pair of neat grays with bells on their bridles. From the windows of the coach Nono could see glimpses of a white landscape laced with black boughs and intermittently a river. A few buildings caught her eye and once or twice another carriage appeared and vanished as quickly as it came into view.

The carriage came to a stop presently and the lady's maid lifted Nono out and set her on her feet in front of a tall house. With this adventure scarcely realized, Nono was swept indoors and almost instantly plunged into a tub of hot water.

Nono was familiar with cold water and with salt water but hot water was something altogether new. Further, the water was full of foam which stung her eyes mercilessly. When she opened her mouth to scream she gulped a good deal of it and it had a strong, not to say violent and disagreeable flavor. Not since Nono's tribe had let out its last war whoop had such a scream come from Nono as when she swallowed a mouthful of soap made of lard and lye and scented with lemon and rosewater. Nono spluttered, choked and shrieked and the lady's maid slapped her, scolding like old Ani but in her own language.

Nono could not know that this drenching was nothing but a bath. She marveled between her outcries that these people had gone to such trouble and brought her such a distance merely for the pleasure of drowning her. But in the end she did not drown. The maid fished her from the tub, dried her off and then undertook to dress her. The dressing was an elaborate process and the clothes which Nono was expected to wear bore no relation to the tattered piece of sailcloth which the woman gave away to another black woman — passing it to her gingerly with a pair of tongs and with an expression of great disgust on her stern, dark face.

The woman put a white embroidered shift on Nono and then a series of petticoats. Nono thought she was being smothered as the petticoats were flung over her head, and fought them like a wildcat. As Tryphena said afterward to Hagar in the kitchen, it was like trying to dress a windmill in a hurricane. She completely lost patience and gave Nono's ears a resounding box.

"Oh, what a wicked little heathen!" exclaimed

Tryphena. "Don't you know that God will punish you for tearing such a fine petticoat? French lace too! Miss Prue only wore it three months before she outgrew it. You don't deserve to have such things, miss, if you don't treat them right."

All of this was of course lost on Nono, who screamed again at the blow and then screamed some more, until she had no breath to scream with because Tryphena now began to lace her into a tight little bodice. Every time Nono drew a breath to scream with Tryphena tugged that much harder at the laces until Nono could only gasp and hiccough. In the midst of this riot the woman of the blue cloak came into the room. She had put off her cloak and was most alarmingly pale, tall, and imperious in a white gown with a blue sash. Even her hair, piled into curls and puffs on top of her head, was white.

By this time, Nono, tightly laced, was standing in the middle of the room, plucking woefully at her petticoats. The tears streamed down her cheeks and she was licking them up as fast as she could. The woman took Nono's hand, drew her over to a chair near a window, and sitting down, began to talk to her.

In spite of the strange words the voice carried meaning to Nono. It was the voice which women use to children from Cape Adamastor to the glaciers of the Arctic Circle and Nono stopped crying to listen. It was long since she had heard such sounds. And the woman had a long, slender neck and large brown eyes like those of an impala doe. Nono grew quiet and let the two women finish dressing her. They put a white frock on her and tied a red sash around her middle. They put stockings and shoes on her feet, making her feel that she had grown a pair of hooves. When she was dressed they put a kerchief around her shoulders and a stiff white cap on her head, tied under the chin with two red ribbons. Then they led her to a looking glass. Nono had often seen her own face looking up at her from the stream near the village but no looking glass had ever come her way. The stranger who faced her from this gleaming surface was a very pleasing and elegant creature. It was a small, wiry personage with sleek, black skin, a little hooked nose, a wide mouth and very large, black eyes, fringed with long lashes. Long, long ago Nono's ancestors had journeyed down from the northeastern part of Africa. On the way down they had intermingled with other peoples, but their children's children still had the look of the long-buried northern cities. Nono, seeing herself in the glass, suddenly remembered her father's hooked nose, fierce mouth and penetrating eyes. The little creature in the glass looked like Nono's chieftain father.

"Why she is a little ebony queen!" declared Nono's new mistress. "Come, little Carthaginian, let us bring you to your master."

She took Nono's hand and led her down a flight of stairs. Nono hesitated at the first stair, uncertain how to approach this contraption, but then, observing her guide, she followed the lady's example cautiously and gained the foot of the staircase without accident. The woman threw open a tall polished door and led Nono into a room.

The room seemed at first to Nono nearly as large as a barracoon — but it bore no other resemblance to a barracoon.

The floor was covered with a pattern of flowers. There

was a grate where a lively fire burned, casting a light and a warmth over the pale green paneled walls. The room was lit with slender wax tapers and was furnished with objects as mysterious to Nono as the African bush and its inhabitants would have looked to the people who lived here. There were sofas, tables, candle snuffers and an embroidered fire screen. There was a black and white spaniel dog, and a spinet near the curtained window with a row of black and white teeth. There were shelves of calf-bound books, pictures on the walls of people and ships and one of a magnificent arrangement of flowers. Nono looked around her and gave vent to a long "Ooooooh!"

Two people occupied places near to the fire, one a man, seated in an armchair, and the other a little girl of about Nono's age who crouched on a footstool at his knee. The man was slender and appeared to be rather elderly. His white hair was gathered into a knot at the back of his head and tied with a length of black ribbon. He wore white satin breeches and white silk stockings. His coat was of bright blue satin, frogged with gold. The lace at his throat and wrist was white as foam. He sat with his face toward the fire but when he turned from the blaze Nono saw that not only his skin, hair and linen were white but even his eyes were white — white as the snow-covered world which she had first seen from the window of the barracoon only this morning.

"Oh, Papa," cried the little girl. "Oh, if only you could see her! She is like a little statue."

This child did not have white eyes. Her eyes were brown and lively and her long red hair flowed down her back. She wore a frock of pink satin, and like Nono she wore white

stockings and black slippers which peeped from under her long shining skirts. Her nose was freckled and when she looked up and smiled Nono saw that she had lost her front teeth.

"So you have brought your shard of black ivory, I gather," said the man. "Have you named your little wench, Mrs. Scrooby?"

"She is called Pansy on the bill of sale, sir," said the woman. "One of the crew is said to have named her. She bears a good character. I do assure you, Mr. Scrooby, that I think her a great bargain. I had her for three pounds. I fancied her, she is so pretty. I had thought to find an older wench but since she is so young she will prove the more biddable. She should train up well for a lady's maid. She was frightened at the journey hither. I had much ado to calm her but I observe that she comforts herself very well now. I have always held that kindness —"

"Pansy," said the man, holding out his hand. Nono took a step towards him. He sat there so still, and looking so straight ahead of him with his white eyes, that it struck her that he required something of her. She had no notion of what it might be and knitted her broad brow in some perplexity, anxious to rise to the occasion. The man continued very still with his hand outstretched. Slowly Nono advanced to his side. When she reached his knee the man passed his hand over her features and then touched her hand.

"So your name is Pansy," the man said.

With his white eyes he had so melancholy an air that Nono was put in mind of her friend the sailor, who had dressed her in sailcloth. She wanted badly to do something for this man — to give him a present. Suddenly an inspiration struck her. She had a lively recollection that in her village the witch doctor had owned a necklace of teeth of which he had been very fond. Teeth! She glanced at the smiling little girl sitting beside the fire and put a finger to her own mouth. She had one good tooth which was very loose. She thought it would come out with one pull. She tried it and out it came. She put it as politely as possible into the man's outstretched hand.

His fingers closed gently over it.

"I think you must be about six years of age," said the man. "Pansy."

"Pansy," said Nono distinctly.

"Oh, Papa," cried the red-haired child, "isn't she clever! She knows her name."

"Pansy," said the man, and touched her face again.

It was clear that the gift of a tooth had brought pleasure and a reward. For the man had made a gift in return. Nono was no longer Nameless. She was expected to answer to the word Pansy and she pronounced it again, savoring it carefully and glancing about the room inquiringly to gauge the effect of her name on these generous strangers. The man, the woman and the child all nodded approval. From that time on, Nono was Pansy to her intimate friends.

It was not long before Pansy discovered that she had a great deal of use for a name and moreover that everything else had a name. Even the spaniel had a name — Mop. At first Pansy had thought that all dogs were mops but she became acquainted with Fido, Towser, Sweetheart and Jess, who all responded to their names and thus gave her a high opinion of the intelligence of dogs.

Being without a name in New Haven, Connecticut Colony, which was where Pansy's fortunes had brought her, would have been like being a pot without a handle. Her name was in constant use. "Pansy" was on somebody's tongue from morning till night. Somebody was always giving her instructions or sending her to fetch something or simply addressing her.

The family who had bought Pansy was named Scrooby. The white-eyed man was Squire Scrooby of Scrooby's Acres and his wife was Madam Scrooby and the child was Prudence Rebecca Scrooby, whom the servants called Miss Prue. The servants, of whom there were four in the house and three more who worked in the stables, were all of Pansy's color, save one somewhat lighter who, she learned, was an Indian — whatever that might be. But unlike Pansy they had all been born in the New World. Only their mothers had come on slave ships and none of them save possibly the Indian had ever seen their fathers. Pansy was secretly rather proud that she knew who her father was and what he had been in his lifetime. She was glad that she had been born in Africa instead of on the slave ship.

Two of the servants were women: Tryphena, Madam Scrooby's maid, who was also nurse to Prudence, and Hagar, who cooked. Then there was Hannibal, the coachman and farm manager for Mr. Scrooby; John, who attended at table; Prince, who helped him; Peter, the Indian, who gardened; and Reuben, who did everything else. Reuben might almost have preferred to have had no name at all since it was in such constant use. All day long and often during the night someone was calling Reuben.

"Reuben, fetch in the wood, Reuben, light the candles,

Reuben, harness up the horses, fetch my snuffbox, bring the coals, polish the brasses, shovel the snow, clean the shoes."

Pansy's first weeks in the white world of the Scroobys were frighteningly complicated. Words tumbled off people's tongues and she had to piece them together into sense and learn to make suitable answers, a task which took all her time and strength. Then there was the matter of time itself. There was a time of day, a time of the week, of the month, and as she later discovered, of the year. And the days, the months, the years had names. The names of the days and of the months changed but the year remained the same — at least for a while, turning green with spring and summer, scarlet and gold in autumn and white in winter. Pansy was much impressed with this clever climate. But the year continued to be Anno Domini 1775. Time ticked away in the great tall clock in the parlor. The clock knew when the sun would rise and when it would set. It rang to summon the family to meals and to prayers. Day and night it chimed away the hours. Like Pansy it had come from over the sea — from a land called England. Mr. Scrooby's great-grandfather had brought it with him when he had crossed the ocean nearly a hundred years before. It had ticked away the lives of many Scroobys. It would tick away the lives of Prudence and Pansy and of their children and their children's children. Once every seven days Madam Scrooby took a great key and wound up the clock. Every day Pansy took a stool and a dustcloth, mounted the stool, and dusted the clock until the glass that framed its face shone. Otherwise it took care of itself.

Almost as soon as she could speak at all, Pansy was

taught spells and incantations, or so she regarded the words and phrases which she was obliged to repeat daily to Madam Scrooby until she had got them by heart. She had no bones to rattle as she would have had in Africa but she assumed that she must be learning New Haven magic until Madam Scrooby somewhat sharply undeceived her. She was learning the catechism and the customary prayers, explained Madam Scrooby, without which she could not hope to become a Christian. Pansy nodded. Madam Scrooby went on explaining and Pansy went on nodding — and for weeks — until she was clear that she was supposed to glorify God and enjoy Him forever, to be content in the condition to which God had called her and that she was made of dust; the same dust, no doubt, which collected on the clockface. It was clever, she thought, of God to find a use for it, since people couldn't wait to get rid of it. She polished the clock diligently, an occupation which bored her, and solaced her tasks by occasionally running her fingers over the keys of the spinet.

Pansy had learned within her first week in the new world that the spinet in spite of its teeth was harmless, and was, in fact, no more than a rather magnificent kalimba.

Along with religion Pansy Scrooby learned manners. She was instructed in the use of knives and forks, goblets and napkins. She learned modes of address, and how to curtsy, an art which she practiced before the looking glass until she had achieved a graceful obeisance which would have done credit to a countess, so Madam Scrooby said. Tryphena observed that the little savage gave herself airs.

"Are you planning to visit the King?" she laughed

scornfully. "Don't forget to remember me to him when you do your season at court."

But many of the things that Pansy learned, although different in kind from what she had begun to learn in Africa as a tiny child, had to be learned for much the same reasons. In this country, too, it was necessary to keep the rules in order to stay out of difficulties. Pansy learned to keep out Tryphena's way when she was doing up lace ruffles with hot irons. She walked in wide circles when Hagar was cooking large dinners. She learned how to cross a New Haven street without falling under the wheels of carriages and wagons. The means to safety were the opposite of those used in the bush — instead of mingling with the shadows Pansy let herself be seen. But apart from clocks, snow, cobbled streets, spaniels, spinets, tall-steepled churches and lace ruffles Pansy could have pointed to many things in New Haven that were not so very different from African things. In New Haven she was pleased to learn that they poured water to the god whom they worshipped.

The water pouring was part of the naming ceremony. They had had a naming ceremony in Africa but it was noisier and more amusing than the New Haven variety. Squire and Madam Scrooby, with Prudence, took Pansy to the church and held a naming ceremony. The priest, whose name was Mr. Stiles, was a combination witch doctor and chief. He poured water over Pansy and gave her the names of Sophia Cecilia. But nobody ever called her by these splendid names until much later in life. The names were Mr. Scrooby's choice. He selected Sophia because this name means wisdom and Mr. Scrooby had early formed the opinion that Pansy was going to be a wise woman. He thought so because she made such rapid progress in the English language. She labored to speak precisely as he did, mimicking his tones of voice and choice of words until she had his accent perfectly. He called her Cecilia because he entertained a passion for music. When he heard Pansy warbling a little catch-tune as she fingered the spinet, fancying herself alone and out of her master's earshot, he told his wife that Pansy might grow up to be a singer.

"She sings as true as a wood thrush," he remarked to Madam Scrooby. "Our little savage is full of music." He called Pansy to his chair and told her about the musician Cecilia, and repeated some poetry to her. He declaimed:

> *Let old Timetheus yield the prize,*
> *Or both divide the crown.*
> *He raised a monarch to the skies,*
> *She drew an angel down.*

Pansy praised the poem and Mr. Scrooby asked her which she would prefer to do.

"Which what?" asked Pansy.

"Raise a mortal to the skies or draw an angel down," said her master.

"Both," said Pansy, "sir." Mr. Scrooby laughed immensely and afterwards told Madam Scrooby that Pansy would "go far." Pansy happened to overhear him and marveled inwardly that she had come so far already.

As a result therefore of Mr. Scrooby's views on her character Pansy was baptized Sophia Cecilia with the Scroobys standing godparents to her, promising to shield her from the world, the flesh and the devil and to see that she was received into the congregation of the First Church in New Haven at a later time.

When Pansy first arrived at the Scroobys she had been put to sleep on a mat in a little attic where Hagar slept. She found it lonely there, for Hagar came to bed very late and Pansy was often awake in the dark for many hours. She wept for loneliness in the slow passage of time between eight o'clock and midnight. She had never been so comfortable or so well cared for in her life and she had nothing to dread but Tryphena's sharp tongue; she cried because this safety in itself was strange, clinging to Prudence when bedtime approached. Prudence was as unwilling to part from Pansy as Pansy could have wished, so Madam Scrooby took her away from the attic and put her to sleep on a cot in a closet off Prudence's bedchamber. Still Pansy cried silently, and sometimes in her sleep, until Madam Scrooby put a rushlight in her room which burned all night like a little star and Pansy was comforted and slept at ease.

After several months, when Pansy had got her tongue around the names of all the objects in the house and could pronounce nearly everything that she wished to say, Madam Scrooby began to teach her a few accomplishments. She taught her to knit, to sew a plain seam, to embroider flowers on a napkin, to polish silver and to keep the keys of the spinet white and shining.

Pansy longed to know how to make the spinet sing and Madam Scrooby assured her that if she were very good she might be permitted to learn. It would be a shame, said Madam Scrooby, to allow real talent to go to waste. She talked less and less of making a chambermaid of Pansy, and more and more of making her a musician.

Pansy tried hard to be good, and succeeded. It was important to be good in New Haven. In Africa there had been no talk of being good. The rules had to be kept but beyond this nobody asked any questions. But more and more it dawned on Pansy that in New Haven they talked of little else, although they continued to behave much as the others whom she had observed in her travels.

In New Haven they were much oppressed by their god. He was, she learned, a very uncomfortable god to get along with. He insisted upon people's being good but did nothing to help them improve as far as Pansy could see. In fact he made things harder. He was bad-tempered, jealous and vengeful, all the things that his people were supposed not to be. The only pleasure he had was in seeing people sit for hours together telling him how wonderful he was or listening to Mr. Stiles tell them how dangerous he was. And even then he did nothing to put an end to bad weather or to relieve the troubles of the poor. In this respect he did not greatly differ from the rulemaker in Africa for whom the witch doctor had danced so tirelessly. If everyone sat in church long enough something was bound to happen and then Mr. Stiles said it was because the great, terrible, jealous god was pleased. Pansy found it somewhat discouraging but she pursued goodness anyway. It seemed unfair, however, that Prudence, who was the opposite of good, was to learn how to make the spinet sing as soon as a music master could be engaged.

## CHAPTER 5

*In which Pansy discovers some of the shadows of Divine things, as expressed by Mr. Edwards, and attempts to bring a sinner to repentance.*

RUDENCE REBECCA SALTONSTALL SCROOBY was one of the most spoiled and disobedient children ever to live in New England. All New Haven spoke of her dreadful behavior. Many people considered her to be irretrievably lost. Pansy sometimes thought that the custom they had of naming people in Africa was much more sensible than the one followed in the colonies. For when people named a child in Africa they had had it long enough to know what kind of a person it was and therefore called it something appropriate. If the Scrooby family had waited they could not have had their daughter christened Prudence. They would have called her Daughter of the Storm or Mistress Hurricane or Limb of Satan, which was what the servants called her behind her back.

Prudence had discovered early in life that her parents doted on her with an almost sinful extravagance. Mr. Stiles indeed had remonstrated with them frequently on the subject. They made an idol of the child, he said. The discovery gave Prudence great satisfaction.

"If they hadn't me," she said to Pansy, "they would have nobody. I may do as I please."

So she did as she pleased. When Tryphena dressed her in

the morning she fretted and scolded and pulled off her petticoats and stamped on them and sometimes slapped the lady's maid.

"You are a very wicked girl, Miss Prue," said Tryphena, "and if you take on so the devil will come and carry you away to the eternal fire. Oh, you'll be sorry then with not a drop of water to cool your naughty tongue."

"I don't care," said Prudence. "I like to be wicked."

When Mr. Stiles, who had poured water on Pansy, came to call, Prudence was rude about his red face, his wig, his short, bandy legs and his rusty gown. "Like a crow," whispered Prudence. "Caw, caw, caw. Flapping through the rain like an old, lame crow."

When she was sent for to the parlor she put her finger in her mouth, pouted and wouldn't curtsy although emphatically ordered to by Madam Scrooby. Pansy shuddered to think what would have happened to anyone who had behaved in such a way to the witch doctor. It would have taken a great deal of dancing to undo that mischief.

"You are a wicked child, Miss Prudence," said the parson. "Don't you know where the wicked go when they die? They go to Hell."

Prudence told Pansy after Mr. Stiles had left that she didn't care a farthing. She certainly didn't want to go anywhere that the parson was going anyway.

"And Heaven sounds horrid," said Prudence. "Just like church only it goes on forever and every day is Sunday. Mr. Stiles is going there. Everyone agrees to that."

"But how can they tell?" asked Pansy.

"He's one of the Elect," said Prudence. "He can't help it, any more than you can help being black. He was always going to Heaven, even from the beginning of time. It doesn't matter what he does. He could be as wicked as the worst heathen and he would still go to Heaven. It's been ordained."

The following day being Sunday, Pansy paid rather close attention to the sermon which Mr. Stiles preached, in the hope of learning something of the Elect. On previous Sundays she had allowed her mind to ramble during the discourse but on this particular day she listened carefully and learned a good deal, to her great discomfort. The New Haven god was terribly out of sorts that morning and it seemed that everyone was about to catch it. Only the Elect would be spared and these were so very few in number that they scarcely seemed to matter. As for the heathen and those laboring in darkness — there was no hope at all.

Outside the windows of the church the snowflakes whirled among the black branches of the trees. Pansy and Prudence both held hot stones wrapped in flannel but they cooled down during the sermon in spite of all the sizzling and frying going on in the pulpit. Mr. Stiles pleaded with the congregation to rid itself of its heart of stone and be saved. Pansy wondered anxiously how to do this and Prudence, who had been squirming for the last hour, dropped her stone to the floor with a crash that brought the beadle from his nap with a terrible start. He advanced upon the Scrooby pew with his wand upraised, while Prudence and Pansy cowered and whimpered and Mr. Stiles, after one furious pause, went on relentlessly. Sin was everywhere, he whispered. Yes, everywhere, he exclaimed with a shout that brought every head in church up straight. He returned again to the Elect. There were none present for

certain, save perhaps himself. The sinners in church rustled uncomfortably. Pansy wondered if it was because of her wickedness that she had been sent to the slave ship. At least it was something of a comfort to know that she was no longer a heathen but had been baptized and was, in fact, now sitting in the only true church. It distressed her to think that so few people had this privilege. Glancing around the building she noticed that all the Scrooby household were here with the exception of Peter. His absence made her very uneasy.

After the sermon there was, as usual on Sundays, a very large dinner. Pansy was thoughtful but Prudence ate a good deal of ham and chicken and apple pie and said she didn't believe in Hell. But that night after she had been put to bed in her great four-poster bed with its white ruffled curtains and patchwork quilt she began to scream and said that she had changed her mind. She believed in Hell. Pansy sprang from her own little bed, seized the candle and ran into Prudence's room.

"Prudence, oh, Miss Prue, why do you scream?" exclaimed Pansy.

"I'm screaming because I'm such a wicked girl and must go to Hell when I die," roared Prudence. "Oh, oh, oh, I've broken the Sabbath and made a graven image of Mr. Stiles and been saucy to my parents. That's three commandments in a row. All broken to bits!"

"Oh dear," said Pansy. "What must we do to be saved?"

"It's nearly impossible," said Prudence. "You heard Mr. Stiles yourself. Hardly anyone can be saved. Everyone is doomed. I don't mind so much during the day but it's dreadful at night. Oh, oh, oh!"

To comfort her Pansy climbed into bed with Prudence and took her in her arms. This seemed to soothe poor Prue and she went off to sleep but Pansy lay awake a great while thinking and worrying about the heathen and the Elect. If Mr. Stiles were to be believed, the Elect were in for rather a lonely time of it.

Honesty compelled her to admit that it was very unlikely that Prudence was of the Elect, for in spite of her nightmares she was not sufficiently afraid of Hell to alter her ways. She complained of her food, she pounded the spinet with her fist, she unwound the wool from Tryphena's distaff, she stepped deliberately in puddles with her best slippers on, she tore her fine reading book, *The Day of Doom,* with the interesting pictures of The Last Judgment which had been sent her by relatives in Litchfield. Several of the pages were lost and Madam Scrooby forbade Prudence to read any book but the Bible for a week. This made very little difference to Prudence, who couldn't read anyway.

Since Prudence certainly was not of the Elect Pansy wondered with more and more anxiety who was. The more she thought about it the more the question vexed her. Her worries increased daily in fact because she could not bear to think that anyone whom she knew should not be of the Elect. Surely something could be done. She must ask someone how the problem was to be solved. Prudence must be saved first, of course, and then she would turn her attention to the others. Saving Prudence proved really more than she was equal to. It turned out to be impossible to save someone who was only damned at night. For in the mornings Prudence usually informed Pansy that she had changed her mind again and was one of the Elect.

"But how can you know?" asked Pansy.

"I feel it here," said Prudence, pounding her chest. "The Elect *know.* I'm a child of light. Don't tease me. Go and save someone else."

Pansy thought that this would be a splendid thing to do but could not think whom to begin with.

"Tryphena," she asked, "are you saved?"

"Why what a question!" exclaimed Tryphena. "Certainly I'm saved. Why shouldn't I be?"

"I was wondering," said Pansy, "since Mr. Stiles tells us that the Elect are very few."

"Oh, he wasn't talking about me," said Tryphena. "I was converted years ago. I was convenanted at sixteen and so was Hagar."

"And Hannibal?" asked Pansy.

"Certainly," said Tryphena — Hannibal was her husband. "You don't suppose I should be married to one of the doomed. Hannibal is of the Elect."

"And John and Prince and Peter and Squire and Madam Scrooby?"

"What sort of people do you take us for?" snapped Tryphena. "Squire and Madam Scrooby indeed! I never heard of such impudence."

"And Prudence?"

"I shouldn't be too sure if I was Miss Prue," said Tryphena, "and I couldn't answer for Peter, I'm sure. He's an Indian. He doesn't attend our church. No, I can't say for Indians. He's likely a vessel of wrath. I shouldn't be amazed to know it."

"But could he not be saved too if he really longed for salvation?" asked Pansy. It seemed grossly unfair that Peter should be left out.

"He's got a heart of stone," said Tryphena. "I doubt he could be converted. He is always very saucy when he's sent for the eggs by Hagar. Now run along. You ask too many questions. The sooner you get over that habit the better it will be for you, my girl. You have plenty of work to do without worrying if your betters are of the Elect. And I have ironing to do, so take yourself off."

Pansy took herself off. Tryphena's certainty was somewhat comforting, save in the case of Peter. She could see him from the window of the pantry where she had wandered, leaving Tryphena to her linens. Peter was coming from the barn carrying a harness. He took the harness to a stone in the middle of the barnyard, sat down on the stone and began to oil the harness.

Pansy fetched her cloak, slipped out the pantry door and walked over to Peter. It seemed her duty to try to save him since nobody else in the household either needed or wished for salvation.

Now that she was actually with Peter she did not know very well how to begin. It was rather early in the morning and perhaps he was not wide awake enough to be saved. He had a rather sleepy look at all times and spoke very seldom to anyone.

"Ahem," said Pansy.

Peter looked up for a moment and then looked down and continued to polish the harness.

"Ahem," said Pansy once more.

"Hagar sent you for more eggs?" asked Peter.

"No, thank you," said Pansy. "You may bring them in later. It was something else that I wished to speak to you about."

"What's the matter?" asked Peter. "They flog you?"

"Certainly not," said Pansy. "I am never flogged."

"Good," said Peter. "Not like most."

"Peter," said Pansy, twisting the hem of her apron in her little dark hands, "Peter, are you a heathen?"

"Eh?" said Peter.

"You mustn't be a heathen," said Pansy. "It's very wicked. God will punish you. You should go to the parson and be baptized. You must never bow down to idols. It's terribly dangerous. You must be converted at once."

"I don't want to be converted," said Peter firmly, but looking a little startled, an unusual state for Peter. "I live in New Haven."

"Oh dear," said Pansy. "That isn't my meaning. I was a heathen once but that was long ago in Africa. Now I'm a member of the First Church."

"That's right," said Peter. "One true church right here."

"But if you think so," objected Pansy, "why don't you go to it?"

"Don't need it," said Peter. "Elect have no need of church."

"Are you Elect?" asked Pansy, astonished. "But Tryphena said —"

"Pay no mind to Tryphena," said Peter comfortably. "Tryphena's not Elect."

"Oh yes, she is. She told me so."

"Bragging," said Peter. "I'm Elect. Sincere Christian. Going straight to Heaven. Inheriting the earth. Parson Holmes say so. Years ago. Now you run away. You dirty your dress out here in the yard. I feed the pigs."

He rose and took the harness back to the barn and came out again with two pails of slops for the pigs.

Pansy walked slowly back to the house, letting herself in at the kitchen door.

Prudence was in the kitchen, sitting on a high stool, scraping cake batter from a bowl with a wooden spoon.

"Prudence," said Pansy. "Peter is of the Elect."

"Laws-a-mercy," said Prudence, "how did you find that out?"

"I asked him and he told me. He says that Tryphena is damned, though."

"Fancy that," said Prudence. "Tryphena is sure of salvation. She's always saying so."

"There is nothing for it but to ask Master," said Pansy.

"Oh, I shouldn't do that," said Prudence. "I don't believe he cares."

"Doesn't care?" exclaimed Pansy. "But he listens to Mr. Stiles every Sunday with his own ears."

"Well, ask him if you must," said Prudence, "but he gives very odd answers. You may have a lick of my spoon if you wish."

Pansy took a lick and then went off toward the parlor.

Mr. Scrooby was sitting in his accustomed chair by the fire, drinking tea. Madam Scrooby sat across from him, reading aloud from the paper. Pansy tiptoed into the parlor just as Madam Scrooby put the paper aside and in time to hear Mr. Scrooby say, "Alas, Mrs. Scrooby, I fear there is nothing in it. We are doomed."

"Oh, dear no, sir!" cried Pansy. "Everyone in the house says they are of the Elect. Oh, we can't all be doomed."

"Bless my soul!" cried Mr. Scrooby. "It's Pansy. What ails the child? Who has been chattering nonsense about Election to her?"

"Mr. Stiles — everybody. Peter — you," wailed Pansy.

"I am aware that Mr. Stiles flatters himself that he is of this august company of the Elect," said Mr. Scrooby thoughtfully, "but I do not recollect having tampered with the question myself, Pansy."

"But you said, sir, just now, that we were all doomed."

"Nay, Pansy, I was merely speaking of the war. I have

never presumed to meddle with the inscrutable dispensations of Providence. Madam Scrooby, I fancy that our little wench requires more lively employment than listening to Stiles in church."

"Miss Prudence thinks she is damned at night," protested Pansy.

"I do not believe that your young mistress is damned," said Mr. Scrooby, "not even at night."

"Then are we all to be saved?"

"Yes, all," said Mr. Scrooby. He lifted his fist and brought it down hard on the table that stood at his right hand. "Everyone, that is, save that accursed band of oppressors who lead this country to war, whether we will or not."

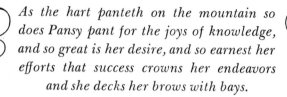

# CHAPTER 6

*As the hart panteth on the mountain so*
*does Pansy pant for the joys of knowledge,*
*and so great is her desire, and so earnest her*
*efforts that success crowns her endeavors*
*and she decks her brows with bays.*

N SPITE of the fact that Prudence behaved like a wild animal a good part of the time, and if there was a Hell stood a fairly good chance of going there, Pansy was immensely fond of her. For Prudence was on the whole a good friend to Pansy. When Pansy had first arrived in the Scrooby home it was Prudence who had taken her by the hand, led her from room to room, and spoken the names of all the things which fell under her eyes. Prudence unwound the distaff to show Pansy what a distaff was. Prudence stole a pot of honey from the larder shelf and hid it under her pillow so that she and Pansy could eat honey in bed. Tryphena had to wash the honey out of their hair and launder all the bed linen and was very angry about it. Pansy was set to extra silver polishing and Prudence was required to write out on a sheet of paper, "Remember not my transgressions nor the sins of my youth," a hundred times. This was the first opportunity Pansy had had to watch anyone write. It struck her as an overwhelming task, in comparison with which her own punishment seemed light, if unsufferably tedious. Prudence, who could not even read as yet, worked and whined and made hen-scratches and blots and eventually had to do the whole imposition twice. It was several days before all the lines were finished to Madam Scrooby's satisfaction and by that time neither Prudence nor Pansy could have told the reason why they had been written in the first place.

In any case it seemed an odd way of reminding a person not to steal honey. But when it dawned on Pansy that all the books in the Scrooby library had been written out in the same impossible way that Prudence had tackled the sins of her youth, she was filled with respect for books. She was therefore profoundly shocked when Prudence tore her reading book, especially since the outrage had been committed in order to see what Tryphena would do about it.

"Why do you make such a fuss?" said Prudence. "There are plenty of books in the house."

"But it is so difficult to make a book," said Pansy. "Look how long it took you to make but a few pages. And there must be marvels in books. Madam reads for hours at a time and never wearies of it. She has a book — it is called *Clarissa Harlowe* — she says it has not its equal and that it would make a stone weep to hear what it has to say. And look how Master listens when Madam reads to him. I should dearly love to know all that happens in books. I should read all day to Master and never tire of it. You are very lucky to be permitted to learn to read."

"But when you grow up you won't have time to read, Pansy," said Prudence. "And when I grow up I shan't plague myself with it either, you may be sure. I shall wear pink frocks with great hoops like Madam Washington and put feathers in my hair and go to balls. I shall visit my cousin, Philadelphia de Lancey, and dance with all her beaux. I shall carry a French fan and all the men will love me."

"What will you talk to them of, if you don't know how to read?" asked Pansy.

"I shan't need to talk to them of anything in particular. I shall be dancing all the night. In Philadelphia there are balls every week. All the finest beaux are there."

"But they will all be old men by the time you are old enough to go to balls."

"I expect there will be some new ones by that time. I certainly can't be expected to dance with old men." Prudence flicked a finger along the spinet keys, making a whirring sound. Pansy stroked a key to soothe it. She gave a small sigh. There were so many things she would have admired to do: to read a book, to play a spinet, and how was she to do them?

Madam Scrooby came into the parlor and said, "Come, come, girls. The devil finds work for idle hands. Prudence, take your slate and practice writing your letters. Pansy, you are neglecting your dusting."

Pansy picked up the feather duster and Prudence made a wry face and fetched the slate. She wrote diligently for a few minutes but presently she whistled up Mop and gave him an old slipper to worry. Then she began to chirp to the canary who lived in a cage which hung in the parlor window. Then she grew weary of that and began to draw funny pictures of Mr. Stiles walking up the aisle in church with the beadle behind him, both looking very solemn and dreary.

Pansy picked up the slate which Prudence had dropped

with the pencil alongside and tried to make some sense of what Prudence had scrawled on it. She started to copy with the pencil the marks which Prudence had made. Then she put the slate down with another small sigh. It was all very well to copy marks on a slate but there was not much profit in it if the marks didn't mean anything.

Madam Scrooby's voice came trilling through the parlor. "It is time for you girls to attend to your samplers."

Prudence and Pansy were both at work on samplers. They were very pretty designs. Prudence's sampler had a picture of a rose tree in the middle of the canvas. Underneath the rose tree stood a sundial. Above the sundial a dove fluttered with an olive branch in its beak. Directly beneath the sundial there was a lamb. At the bottom of the sampler the numbers one through ten made a border. The borders on both sides were made up of the letters of Prudence's full name. Across the top there were more letters. They spelled out: "Remember thy Creator in the days of thy youth." Prudence's age was written out in the upper left-hand corner and the date on which the sampler had been begun was traced in the opposite corner. It was really quite lovely — or would be when Prudence finished it.

Pansy's sampler was also rather charming. In the middle of her canvas there was a green tree which Pansy was now at work on. There was a sun with rays in yellow to be embroidered when she had finished the tree. Then there was a plough to be stitched in black. There were two bluebirds in the tree and around the border there were twenty-six daisies separated from each other by the letters of the alphabet, picked out in scarlet. As in Prudence's sampler the numbers ran along the bottom, and at the top there were the words, "Go to the ant, thou sluggard, consider her ways and be wise." To the left of the picture there was Pansy's full name, Sophia Cecilia Scrooby, and to the right the words: "Ex vinculo Africae aetas suae anni 7 1775." Both of these samplers had been designed by Madam Stiles as a favor to Madam Scrooby. Madam Stiles was learned — Mr. Scrooby said she was "a blue."

Stitching away, Pansy wondered what all these words said. It was clear that they were all made up of bits of the alphabet. If only she could discover how to put all the pieces together they might make sense. Screwing up her smooth round forehead, Pansy stitched and stitched. She stitched at an idea. If she were to copy each letter carefully on the slate after she had stitched it she might conquer the alphabet in this way. Once she had got the alphabet firmly in her head she might set about the task of mixing the letters up into words. Once she had made words on a slate she might be able to read them. And there was certainly no harm in trying. She would abandon the tree and address herself to the letters.

It took Pansy about a month to learn all the letters. She was not permitted to sew on Sundays and was required to sew on all other days, so she worked at the alphabet all through the November of 1775. She had been in America about a year by that time.

Prudence was generous with her slate. She said she hated the slate anyway but during that November she even contrived to learn a few letters herself.

"At last Prudence is making some progress," said

Madam Scrooby. After she had got all the letters, Pansy went to work on the words about the ant in the motto at the top of the sampler. She learned *go* and *to* and *the* and all the useful words which helped connect things with one another. She was pleased when she learned *ant. Sluggard* and *consider* gave her difficulty but she overcame them at last. She wrote them all down as carefully as she had written out the letters of the alphabet. When she had completed this task she went to the library and took down a book in order to see if any of the words she had learned were to be found in it. She was pleased to find *go, to,* and *the* almost immediately and moreover they were in frequent use in this particular book, a large handsome one with its title written in gold letters. Had Pansy been able to read the title she would have known that the book was Foxe's *Book of Martyrs.* She hunted words through Foxe's *Martyrs* as a cat hunts a mouse, pouncing delightedly on every one she knew. She presently became so adroit at this game that she never missed. And she could have read Sophia Cecilia Scrooby anywhere. She even found *Sophia* in another book. In fact in this book Sophia appeared constantly. She asked Mr. Scrooby who this Sophia was who seemed so important and he answered, "the young lady in Mr. Fielding's chronicle of *Tom Jones*."

Then Pansy began the study of *Ex vinculo Africae. Vinculo* was a terrifying word. Pansy couldn't think where it was leading her and she was no wiser after she had learned it. She went to Tryphena and asked her about the word.

"Bless you," said Tryphena, "it must be the language

talked by the wicked Frenchmen. We don't use such expressions here. Run along. You ask too many questions. You will bring bad luck."

"They used to say that in Africa too," said Pansy.

"They say it wherever there are children," said Tryphena. "Children should be seen and not heard."

"Oh, if only I could read!" said Pansy to Prudence.

"You are a tiresome, discontented girl," said Prudence. "And I am not at all sure that you are supposed to learn to read. I expect you aren't, you know. You're supposed to be content in the condition to which God has called you. It says so in the catechism. It doesn't say a word about learning to read."

"It doesn't say a word about not learning to read either," said Pansy. "If God didn't want me to learn to read he should have mentioned it."

"You can't expect him to remember *everything,*" said Prudence. "He probably never thought you would want to. Most people don't. I wish I didn't have to. I think you're well off as you are. I expect you're flying in the face of Providence."

"That is what Tryphena says when you are naughty," said Pansy. "All it means is that you are flying in the face of Tryphena."

Prudence laughed. "If you don't mind, Providence will strike you dead. Tryphena can only slap you. I should be careful if I were you."

"I believe," said Pansy, "that Providence wishes me to learn to read. I must have faith to move mountains like Saint Paul. *Ex vinculo Africae!* I wonder if Saint Paul would have known what that means."

7 0

She took her sampler and went into the kitchen where Madam Scrooby was making mincemeat to put into the Christmas pies. The kitchen smelled deliciously of cinnamon and cloves. The spices bubbled in an iron kettle and Madam Scrooby was rather sticky and hot. She had tied up her hair in a kerchief and looped her skirts above her petticoats. Hagar stooped by the kettle to keep her eye on her pastry which was in the baking oven — a little cabinet in the chimney beside the great fireplace where the joints and fowl were roasted on spits. At this time of year the kitchen somewhat resembled the hold of the Portuguese ship.

Pansy held her sampler up. "Madam, what does that say?" she asked, pointing to the words which troubled her so.

"Something about Africa, child," said Madam Scrooby. "I've little acquaintance with ancient tongues. You must ask your master. He is very learned. He read all of Rector Pierson's *Natural Philosophy* when he was at the College. And he has mastered both the Latin and the Greek."

So when the candles were lit in the evening Pansy took her sampler to the parlor.

"Master," said Pansy, "I should like to know what *Ex vinculo Africae* means. I have been sewing it with beautiful red silk ever since the snow came but I cannot find the words in any of your books. It isn't even in the Bible."

Mr. Scrooby turned his face toward Pansy and seemed to gaze at her with his white eyes.

"Why, what a droll little monkey to be looking for Latin words! Whatever put such a thought in your head?"

"The sampler put it there," said Pansy. "First one word

and then another. When I have sewn a word I search for it in other places. You would be amazed at how often I find them. I have found *go* and *to* and *the* and *and*. Once I even found *sluggard*. All these are common words. I have heard Madam say that Peter and Prudence are both slug-gards. But *Ex vinculo Africae* is different. That is, I under-stand about Africae — although that isn't the way I say it — but the rest is very difficult. Tryphena says I will bring bad luck with all my questions. Many people say this but often you don't agree with everyone else so I thought perhaps you would tell me what it means."

Mr. Scrooby listened very carefully while Pansy talked. When she had finished he turned his face to the fire and sighed.

"Why have you done all this?" he asked.

"Because I should like to learn to read," said Pansy.

"You have gone to a great deal of trouble," said Mr. Scrooby.

"It *is* a great deal of trouble," agreed Pansy, "and for so very few words too. And there are so many more to learn. I shall be an old woman before I have copied out half the words there are in the world. It's very provoking." It crossed her mind that if Providence intended her to learn to read He might have made it a bit easier.

"When I was your age," said Mr. Scrooby, "I had my greatest pleasure in reading. All through the summer days I read in our orchard. I read by the light of the full moon in my student days. It was my pleasure to climb the hills of New Haven with a book in my pocket and idle whole days away a-reading. I did not think I should live never to open a book again. Like you, Pansy, I may not read. Why do you wish to do so?"

"Because there are so many things I desire to know," said Pansy, "and they are all in books. In Africa there were hardly any books, I daresay, and none could be spared for children. But here there are more than enough for everyone so there should be some for me too. Prudence doesn't think I should learn to read. She says I might be flying in the face of Providence. But I don't think so. If I could read, sir, I could read to you."

Mr. Scrooby smiled. "I cannot teach you to read. But I shall speak of it to your mistress. I cannot believe that you would abuse the privilege of learning. You would put your talent to good account, I swear. And you are a baptized Christian." He paused as some uncertainty crossed his mind. The look on his face reminded Pansy of her father when he had warned her of the crocodile. He looked far away and thoughtful.

"I shall think on it, Pansy," he said.

That Christmas Pansy received two presents, a Bible and a slate. Pansy sat down in her little room and began to copy the Bible onto the state. It was a terible task. When she had filled up the slate with as many words as she could copy she had to rub it all out and continue where she had left off. It proved impossible to contain the Bible on one slate though Pansy wrote as small as possible.

Mr. Scrooby spoke several times of engaging a master to teach Prudence and Pansy but it was difficult at this time to find a master. All the students and tutors at Yale College were busy joining the militia and few people took much interest in instructing young ladies. So Pansy did her lessons by herself. And although she often found it dull to write word after word on the slate nevertheless she kept to it.

Sometimes Prudence came and watched over her shoulder to see how she was getting on but since Prudence never attended to anything for more than a few minutes Pansy worked for the most part alone. She came to know the words she studied very well. They became old acquaintances and fairly greeted her when she met them. She played games with them. "How do you do, Mr. *Go?*" and "I trust I see you well, Madam *Also,*" and "Ah, good day to you, *Verily,* where have you been this long time?" Sometimes she punished a difficult and obstinate word by writing it wrong on the slate. She fancied that words hated to be misspelled. It would be like having clothes that didn't fit. One day while going through her Bible Pansy found that she could read almost all of the passage she was copying down so laboriously. There was a troublesome word, *Absalom,* but as she read she learned that Absalom was a person, a prince, with long red hair like Prudence's. Pansy forgot to copy and went on reading, reading about kings and priests and prophets and armies and the God of the Israelites. When Mr. Scrooby found out what Pansy had accomplished he was going to be greatly pleased.

Mr. Scrooby's birthday fell in the spring and since Pansy didn't have a tooth to give him this year — and indeed would have scorned to offer a tooth, as inelegant — she resolved to read to him as a present. Prudence was knitting her father a pair of slippers and Madam Scrooby had sent to Virginia for some choice tobacco and to Boston for a set of books, but nobody had thought that Pansy might wish to give him a present.

April came and with it Mr. Scrooby's birthday. All the snow had melted and the grass in the meadows was coming up green and sweet. The trees feathered out and young lambs gamboled on New Haven Green. Prudence and Pansy went hunting for violets on the night before Mr. Scrooby's birthday that he might enjoy their fragrance.

Prudence and Pansy enjoyed their ramble through the fresh fields with John, the footman, in attendance and Mop describing circles around them and barking at the blue jays who swooped down at him, angered at his noise. The girls had been cooped up through a long winter with little amusement. This had not bothered Pansy, who had been busy teaching herself to read, but Prudence had found it hard to bear. She had been sent for a few weeks after the New Year to Miss Edwards's dame school in order

to learn to read. Prudence had not learned although Miss Edwards had spared no pains in the teaching. She had beaten Prudence's knuckles with a ruler and had put her in the stocks in the schoolroom when she was pert. None of these punishments had improved Prudence in the least. She was as ignorant and saucy when spring came around as she had been in the fall of the year. The only difference was that from having disliked Miss Edwards she now hated her.

"Nasty cross old Quizz," said Prudence. "I daresay she is of the Elect too. Why are all the Elect so very disagreeable? Hell may be a very bad thing but I'm sure I can't say much for Heaven if it is full of Miss Edwardses."

"Now that I can read why can't I be your teacher?" said Pansy. "Perhaps you will learn more easily with me. I shan't beat you. All you need do is copy down the letters that I set for you."

"That might be quite a good idea, Pansy," said Prudence. "I daresay I shall learn to read with you. And it would certainly disoblige Miss Edwards to find that it was you who taught me all along. Papa need not pay her then."

"We can come out of doors when it is fine," said Pansy, "and read together while enjoying the beauties of nature as Master used to do."

She rather hoped that they might enjoy the beauties of nature the following day after the birthday ceremonies but the next morning it rained. The rain slanted down on the grass and lilac buds beat against the windowpanes. The family waited on Mr. Scrooby in the parlor after morning prayers to wish him long life, and Madam Scrooby and Prudence presented their gifts.

Prudence went to her father, curtsied, kissed him and said ,"I've knitted you a pair of slippers, Papa."

"Anything that my little daughter makes for me with her own hands is of the utmost value to her papa," said Mr. Scrooby.

Then Madam Scrooby gave her husband the tobacco and filled his pipe for him. He lit the pipe and drew a long breath. "Blest weed, whose aromatic gales dispense/To Templars modesty, to parsons sense," he said as the smoke wreathed around his powdered head. "I thank you, madam. We might offer some of this to Stiles, I think."

"Oh, fie!" said Madam Scrooby.

Madam Scrooby also gave her husband the books. They were handsome volumes, bound in leather with designs in gold all over the covers. One was called *The Poetical Works of John Milton* and the other was named *Pamela*. The sight of these two books made Pansy feel quite hungry. Mr. Scrooby smoothed their fine calf covers and smiled.

"I have a present for you too," said Pansy.

"And what may that be, little Pansy?" asked Mr. Scrooby. Pansy took up the first book, *The Poetical Works,* opened it in the middle, and read out loud the first words upon which her eyes fell.

"Hence, loathèd Melancholy," read Pansy. "Of Cerberus and blackest Midnight born." And on and on she read, scarcely stumbling over even the largest words. The Scroobys all listened with mouths agape.

Pansy had hoped to please Mr. Scrooby, but even she was astonished at how marked his pleasure was. At first he was all but speechless, but when he found words to vent his delight they were of the most ceremonious kind. He called Pansy a gift of God and a special mercy sent to comfort him in his affliction. He called her to his knee and kissed her tenderly on the brow. Madam Scrooby embraced her as a daughter and declared that God worked wonders. Prudence remarked that she thought that Pansy worked wonders and was bidden to be more reverent. Madam Scrooby took book after book from the shelves and Pansy read passage after passage in a high clear voice, pronouncing the words with care lest there should be any doubt as to their meaning. And that evening Pansy sat on a footstool at Mr. Scrooby's feet and read to him a play by William Shakespeare called *The Tempest*. When she came to difficult words or strange names Mr. Scrooby assisted her in their correct enunciation. But Pansy read very well on the whole and as she became absorbed in the play she read better and better. Mr. Scrooby listened and smiled and when Pansy, rubbing her eyes, closed the book at last, he embraced her again.

"Yours has been a most compassionate gift, Sophia Cecilia," he said, "for it is no less than a pair of eyes."

To Madam Scrooby he observed that it was high time he looked about him for a suitable person to instruct Prudence and Pansy.

## CHAPTER 7

*In which Pansy and Prudence make the acquaintance of an accomplished tutor who undertakes to further their education.*

T WAS ONE THING to look about him and another to discover a schoolmaster, as Mr. Scrooby discovered during that first year of the war. It began to seem that Pansy and Prudence must scramble themselves into an education without help from instructors. Nobody had time to bother with small girls in 1776. Nobody except her parents cared whether Prudence grew up to be a lady or learned to read or even finished her sampler. There was too much work about the farm to be done to attend to samplers. Prudence tossed the sampler into the back of the cupboard in her bedroom and there it stayed for seventy-five years until one of Prudence's great-granddaughters discovered it and finished it. By that time it was a valuable antique. But at the time that Prudence freed herself of the sampler, valuable antiques were of little interest to anyone in New Haven. The colonies were thinking new thoughts. The mad old King of England and Lord North ruled no more. The colonies were gathering themselves together to form a Republic in which there would be no king. At first Prudence and Pansy had believed that General Washington would be king but Mr. Scrooby explained at length and with some signs of distress and in detail that kings would henceforth be dispensed with. The nation would be built upon the model of the Republic of Ancient Rome. This notion appeared to give him some comfort although he frequently remarked on the evils of being English no longer and the serious threats to trade and commerce occasioned by the war. His brow was often gloomy. In the evenings now Pansy read aloud to him passages from the Roman historians, particularly from Pliny and Tacitus. Mr. Scrooby took some pleasure from these works and Pansy rather less than he did. However she read with patience and docility and called forth much praise. Prudence sat on a footstool at her father's feet and stretched and endured agonies from the itches but was not suffered to leave the room. She found the war extremely trying.

Since she could now read so proficiently Pansy was excused from all housework in the mornings and devoted the time to reading aloud to Mr. Scrooby. She read usually from about ten o'clock in the morning, after prayers were concluded, until one o'clock. Then she was required to spend an hour at writing.

"You must learn a clerkly hand, Pansy," said Mr. Scrooby, "and I shall make you my amanuensis."

Pansy found a clerkly hand hard labor. She worked long hours with a goose quill, cutting nibs in all sizes to find a point to suit her. Madam Scrooby was a sharp critic of the performance and Pansy was often three days together at a simple text such as "Vengeance is mine, saith the Lord" or "He shall dash the heads of thy little ones against the stones."

Neither was she allowed to neglect her sampler nor the other pieces of fine sewing which Madam Scrooby looked out for her. She longed for the day when she might play the spinet and fingered its keys whenever a rare moment of leisure came her way. She picked out tunes for herself and yearned for a music master.

Every day it appeared that some luxury was no longer obtainable. There was no more pipe tobacco from Virginia. Sugar ran short and there was no tea to be had. There was more salt beef at dinner and fewer geese and chickens. Madam Scrooby offered what comfort she could by pointing out that things were far worse in Boston than they were in New Haven, but her household could take little pleasure in the troubles of others while the tallow candles sputtered and stank, the beef bred maggots and washing was next to impossible with soap that was more lye than lard.

Everyone was so busy during the spring of 1776 that Prudence and Pansy were left much to themselves, finding what amusement they might in the woods and meadows. Occasionally they treated themselves to an excursion into the little village of Hamden which lay a mile or so to the west of the farm. Hamden possessed a small tavern and Prudence and Pansy could always find entertainment in watching the comings and goings of travelers, the activities of stableboys and horses, and in picking up odd bits of news about the war. The colonists appeared to win constant victories against hopeless odds and it seemed strange that the war was not over almost before it began, to hear the stableboys talk.

"It's sorcery," said the landlord. "Them Hessians don't fight fair. And they drink like devils. Ah, it's a sad war. You didn't see wars like this when I was a boy. Indian fighting it was then. Those were great times, when General Braddock and Colonel Washington fought the Indians. Blood Creek! There was a battle for you."

Pansy and Prudence had heard the story of Blood Creek several times from the landlord and began to move off as he showed signs of telling it again, to make a short tour of the village. They idled for a few minutes in the church porch, smelling the light scent of the purple and white althea bushes which flowered about the door. They stopped to watch the pewterer at his task of pouring the hot metal into a mold to make spoons. The village was almost empty on this afternoon, a Friday, and the stocks were vacant of thieves, vagabonds and scolds. However there was something of interest pinned to the saddler's door. It was a handbill displaying a picture of a striped and catlike animal. Pansy read the sign aloud to Prudence.

"Unparalleled spectacle," said the sign, "exhibited by Signor Antonio. The gargantuan African tiger. The only one in captivity. Captured by Signor Antonio under conditions of barbaric splendor and with unexampled heroism. The valiant hunter may be seen with the fabulous beast in Shem Sykes's barn. Admission sixpence." Below the sign there was another announcement. "Portraits painted. Three shillings. Sixpence extra with the tiger."

Prudence was all for running off to see the tiger and to have her portrait painted but neither she nor Pansy had sixpence, let alone three shillings. They returned to the tavern in the hope that the landlord might favor them with a loan of sixpence until tomorrow but he refused them.

"I'm a very poor man," he said, "all along of the new

religion. Time was you would see the stocks full of a morning — disorderly conduct. But now folks have turned from the taverns. Too much psalm singing around here for my liking. It's bad for business. The parson over yonder is newfangled and you never hear a good old-fashioned sermon any more. It's all temperance and good works. An honest man can't scrape up a living among folks who drink nothing but water. It's flying in the face of Providence. What was good enough for Parson Edwards ought to be good enough for us. What a sermon he preached! He would send men to cool their tongues fast enough when the Sabbath was over. I mind I went down to Enfield once. Heard him preach the Enfield sermon. Three women fainted. I saw a man fall to his knees and whimper like a baby to be saved. But these new people! They drink milk and ruin an elected man's trade."

"If we come back with sixpence tomorrow may we see the tiger?" asked Prudence.

"Oh, aye. And you may take a handful of these bills to let your friends know that the tiger may be seen hard by the sign of the Eagle of Freedom. My spring ale is at its best and I've still some fair rum."

Pansy and Prudence took the bills and returned with them to the farm. They met nobody in their way and so were unable to spread the news to anyone but Tryphena who said she took little stock in tigers.

"However," she said, "if Madam will allow you sixpence I daresay you may see him. Master has said that Hannibal and I must go to Hamden tomorrow to see what we may do toward procuring another pig. I am to sell the gray goose. We will do better to put down more bacon against next winter and let the goose go. We may as well see the tiger while we are at the market. It is one of the wondrous works of God. I wonder how many people it has eaten. I hope it is well chained."

Madam Scrooby had no objection to allowing the girls sixpence although she would not part with three shillings for a portrait.

They accordingly set off for Hamden quite early on Saturday morning, a fine, chirping day, as Prudence remarked, listening to the thrushes pouring their liquid notes from every tree. Pansy supplied the liquid notes. Prudence said she didn't hear a drop of liquid.

War or no war, it was a busy Saturday in Hamden. Tryphena and Hannibal had gossips there and were soon caught up in discussions of harnessing, beehives, patchwork quilts, new babies, shortages, pickles and deaths. The tavern was as lively as several farmers could make it in spite of the frowns and wry mouths of their womenfolk, and even the stocks were occupied. A fellow had been taken in drink on the previous night and had started a fight. He was sitting with his feet in the stocks, sound asleep and snoring gently in the sunlight.

"Poor thing," said Pansy. "He'll be thirsty when he awakes. We should fetch him some water."

"La," said Prudence. "He's being punished, Pansy. Why he'll only go and do it again if you go running errands for him." Nevertheless she paused to look more closely at the prisoner. He was a young man and quite handsome although at the moment he was in a state of some disorder. He had a fine crop of dark curls without powder and as splendid a moustache as the girls had ever seen. His coat

was made of dark green velvet, the lace at his throat and wrists was fine as Mr. Scrooby's lace although it was dirty, and he wore silk stockings which had clearly once been white. He had silver buckles on his shoes and a gold ring with a red stone on one of his long, tapering fingers.

"Perhaps we'd better fetch him something to drink after all," said Prudence, after a long, wistful look. "One never can tell. He might be a prince in disguise. One hears of such things every now and then."

Pansy nodded her head in its straw sunbonnet and made her way back to the tavern. There she curtsied so sweetly and complained so prettily of thirst that the potboy drew her a measure of cider which she explained must be shared with a friend. Having secured the cider she wended her way back to the stocks. By this time the prisoner had awakened and the constable had come to set him free.

"A bad business, young man," the constable was saying. "Where do you expect to go when you die if you spend your evenings in taverns? That was no way to comport yourself. Drinking and knocking down honest farmers. God will send a mad bull to gore you if you go giving people black eyes."

"A very small sin, my good man," replied the prisoner, "compared to some sins I have seen, a positive act of virtue. Also I have atoned. Oh what a cramp I have in my legs! What happened? How do I come to be in the stocks? Surely nobody would put me here for drinking that infernal rum! Rather the landlord should be here."

"You knocked Farmer Sykes down — him as is taking care of your tiger. It was a very ungenteel way to reward his hospitality."

"Farmer Sykes is a very ungenteel fellow. He says my tiger is not a tiger. And now I remember I did not knock him down. I merely pulled his nose. My tiger is the finest tiger in captivity and comes straight from the jungles of Africa. I challenge Farmer Sykes — swords or pistols — to tell me he does not. God save us! My poor tiger! Who fed my tiger this morning? He is locked in Sykes's barn. I must attend to him at once. Lord, how thirsty I am!"

"We have some cider for you," said Pansy shyly. "We thought you might be thirsty."

"What? Who the dickens are you? Thank you extravagantly." The man took the cider and downed it at a gulp.

86

"Ha! That is very good. Here is a real Christian! Not one of your ranting, canting hedge-preachers who have nothing to offer a man but water — or brimstone. Thank you, little maid. You have a kind and pitying heart. I see you too hail from Africa — like my tiger. *She* will tell Farmer Sykes not to meddle with matters which he knows not of."

"Now, sir," said the constable, "there is the little matter of the fine."

"Put it to my account at the tavern, my dear constable. I must go to my tiger."

"There is also the matter of the six pullets, sir," said the constable. "If you recall, you knocked Farmer Sykes down because he accused the tiger of eating six pullets. A serious charge in wartime, sir."

"A serious charge and unfounded," replied the man. Now that he was released from the stocks he began to look much better and had assumed a haughty air which became him well and seemed to intimidate the constable. "Would my tiger stoop to mere pullets? A creature which gorged itself on elephant and giraffe and consumed a dozen ostriches without waiting for the cloth to be removed! No, my dear man. It was a fox which ate those pullets."

"If the tiger is such a bold tiger I am surprised that he didn't eat the fox too," said the constable.

"My tiger would not condescend to attack a fox. He is too chivalrous."

During this conversation Pansy and Prudence were listening with their mouths wide open. The stranger had a delightful way of talking, trilling his r's and, now that his hands were free of the stocks, making exciting gestures. Prudence and Pansy could fairly see the tiger gobbling up elephants as fast as he could swallow them. Clearly this lively fellow was the Signor Antonio whose name appeared on the handbill.

"Oh, sir!" exclaimed Prudence, "Won't you let us see the tiger?"

"For sixpence, my dear young lady, you may gaze upon the tiger all day. Let me see your sixpence and you shall see the tiger."

Pansy and Prudence produced their sixpences. "Here is the money," said Prudence rather grandly. "Papa has plenty."

"Ah," said Signor Antonio, sweeping the coins into his pocket. "So. You may certainly see the tiger. In return for this favor perhaps I may see the papa. Who, may I ask, is this papa with so much money?"

"He is Squire Scrooby," said Prudence. "We live a little way from here. We came to market today with Tryphena and Hannibal to buy a pig."

"Your papa must indeed have a great deal of money if he proposes to buy a pig," said Signor Antonio. "Pigs are very dear. I doubt if one can be afforded. You might however buy my tiger."

"Buy the tiger!" gasped Prudence. "But I'm afraid that even Papa couldn't buy a tiger. Why he would cost pounds and pounds and pounds."

"Two pound ten would do it," said Signor Antonio. "Cheap at the price and much more beautiful than a pig. Here is what I shall do. Since I am tired of town life, I shall quit Hamden and pay a visit to your farm with the tiger. I shall dine there and discuss the matter. I shall sell

88

you the tiger and what is more I shall paint your portrait — all for three pounds and dinner. What do you say?"

"Oh I should love it of all things," said Prudence. "We keep very little company these days. It's the war that keeps people from visits. Oh, do come to dinner. And you must paint Pansy's portrait too."

"I shall paint your friend's portrait with extreme pleasure. Do you think your papa will pay for both portraits?"

"Mamma said we were not to commission a portrait," said Prudence, "but I shall ask Papa. He buys me anything I wish. And perhaps Mamma won't mind if we give it to her after it is painted. We have many portraits at home but they are all of grandparents and aunts. There isn't one of Pansy and me. Mamma has always said she would like to have one taken. She says she would like to hire Mr. Copley or Mr. West to do it."

"I should do it much cheaper than Mr. Copley or Mr. West," said Signor Antonio persuasively. "That should please your papa."

"I forgot to mention that Papa is blind," said Prudence. "He won't much care for a portrait himself but I daresay he would be glad to have it cheaper."

"If your papa is blind he will certainly prefer my portraits to those of Mr. Copley or Mr. West. And we shall make a wonderful surprise for your mamma. We shall tell her nothing of them until the portraits are done. Your papa will be forced by her delight in them to buy several. I shall paint the whole farm — with my tiger in it. The tiger and the lamb shall lie down together. After the tiger has been shown to the enthusiastic multitude I shall bring him to your farm. I might remind you that this tiger has been shown to crowned heads. Kings and queens have shuddered at his ferocious appearance."

"Pansy and I won't shudder," said Prudence cheerfully. "I don't suppose we shall be afraid of a tiger."

"This is the gentlest of tigers," said Signor Antonio, contradicting himself flatly. "You have nothing to dread. He wouldn't harm a fly."

"I thought you said he ate elephants," said Pansy.

"So he does, when he can get them. But that is seldom. He will eat anything put in front of him. He has the best of manners and he adores music."

"Oh, so do I," said Pansy.

"All persons of breeding and cultivation adore music," said Signor Antonio. "I myself am enraptured with it. Music hath charms to soothe the savage beast, as the poet says."

"Oh, sir," cried Pansy, "are you a musician as well as a painter?"

"Of course," said Signor Antonio. "I play and sing like an angel."

"Oh, then — perhaps you could teach us," said Pansy. "We have no music master nor any teacher at all just now."

"You are in need of a schoolmaster?" asked Signor Antonio in a businesslike tone.

Prudence said "No" and Pansy said "Yes."

"I have a small matter to discuss with the constable," said Signor Antonio. "I shall come to you at sundown. I should be delighted to become your tutor. Until then, farewell. My compliments to your papa."

He disappeared in the direction of the tavern and Pansy and Prudence went in search of Hannibal and Tryphena whom they found preparing to leave Hamden after a disappointing morning.

Tryphena talked about the sinfulness of the times. There were no pigs to be had at any price and nobody would buy the goose for what Mr. Scrooby was asking for it.

Squire Scrooby was equally disappointed to learn of the poor state of the market.

"Times are very bad," he remarked to Hannibal. "We shall do worse this winter than last if we cannot somehow come by another pig."

"Cheer up, Papa," said Prudence. "Pansy and I have just bought a tiger. He cost only two pounds ten. Surely that is better than a pig."

"You are an innocent and silly child, Prudence," said Mr. Scrooby, "or I should chide you for making a mockery at such a time."

Prudence knew better than to argue with Mr. Scrooby when his voice took on this note of disapproval. She and Pansy beat a quiet retreat from the parlor, leaving Mr. Scrooby to lament with Hannibal over the lack of a pig. They wandered into the kitchen garden in some anxiety over their new pet.

"I'm afraid Papa doesn't quite understand about the tiger," said Prudence.

"But if Mr. Antonio should turn out to be a music master," said Pansy, "perhaps he would feel differently. I do believe he is coming now. Didn't he tell us that he would come at sundown?"

Prudence looked toward the lane beyond the garden. "I

see someone," she said. "But I don't see the tiger. Wait a minute. He is carrying something. If that is a tiger it must be rather small."

The person drew nearer and appeared to be Signor Antonio. He was carrying a good many things, among them a wicker basket which seemed to be quite heavy. Besides the basket he had a pack on his back, and a sack slung over his shoulder which bulged with all sorts of objects. He also carried a staff to help him on his journey. It was obvious that he had more than he could manage and Pansy and Prudence ran down the path between the onion rows to help him.

When they reached him they were delighted to find that the tiger was indeed in the basket. Peering through the slits, they could see that the tiger was a largish, dusty-brown animal, similar to a cat, with sharp ears and green eyes. Its coat was shadowed with faint stripes.

Signor Antonio seemed relieved to see the girls and gladly allowed them to lead him into the kitchen garden.

"There," he said, putting the cage down between two beds of onions. "I fear you have done little to earn your keep today. You should roar louder. People will not pay to see a tiger who does nothing but mew. Three shillings and a few farthings are all you have earned me on market day. Barely enough to pay my fine. How do you expect to live on three shillings a day?"

"Tryphena," shouted Prudence, "Hagar, here is a lovely little African tiger."

Tryphena came to the kitchen door. She looked furious.

"We've no time for mountebanks, my man," she said, "so be off before I call my master. If you're trying to sell my young lady a polecat for two pounds ten it's the stocks for you again."

Hagar also appeared at the door and said, "Now if he had a pig —"

"Polecat!" exclaimed Signor Antonio. "This is one of the finest of African tigers, captured in circumstances of deadly peril amidst cannibals and crocodiles. I assure you he is worth every penny of two pounds ten."

"Gammon!" said Tryphena. "Be off or I shall sweep you out with the broom."

"But —" began Signor Antonio.

"Don't but me," said Tryphena," and get out of my husband's onion patch."

Signor Antonio looked very unhappy. He stooped down and began to talk with the tiger through the slits in the basket.

"Poor tiger," he murmured. "They do not welcome you or your master. The longer I live the more heartless I find the world." He must have done something to the fastening on the basket for suddenly the lid came off and out sprang the tiger. He was small but he looked able to take care of himself in a heartless world. He gave a yowl and leaped across the onions into the cabbage patch. From there he bounded onto the cucumber frames, breaking several, cleared the bean vines, and with one more leap was in the hen yard.

"Help!" screamed Hagar. "There is a tiger in the hen yard!" She and Tryphena rushed out of the kitchen. Peter and Reuben, who were milking, ran up from the barn waving rakes and shovels. John, in knee breeches and stock, his hair half powdered, came from the dining room with Prince, and Hannibal at top speed darted from the parlor and through the kitchen, catching up the musket which adorned the chimneypiece and crying over his shoulder, "Remain where you are, madam. The Hessians have attacked."

The tiger pranced about the hen yard, snarling and pouncing. The air was full of squawks and white feathers. Prudence and Pansy jumped up and down and shrieked. Tryphena and Hagar shook their aprons and screamed, "Scat!"

"Stop him! He is eating the Leghorns!" wailed Tryphena.

"I will stop him," said Signor Antonio, "if you will give me a dinner."

"I will give you anything!" said Tryphena. "Only get that murderer out of our hen yard."

"Fetch me a quilt and I will capture him," said Signor Antonio soothingly. Both girls made a rush for the nearest bedroom, which was at the head of the kitchen stairs, and returned in time to see Hannibal fire the musket, which struck terror to the hearts of all save the tiger. He apparently had guessed that it was not loaded, and continued to eat the Leghorn hen which he had caught.

The report from the musket brought Madam Scrooby to the kitchen garden and, unbeknownst to her, Mr. Scrooby himself. Neither of them had put much faith in the British invasion but they were both curious to know what Hannibal had shot. Signor Antonio turned in this moment of crisis to Mr. Scrooby, whose blind imposing presence filled the kitchen doorway. Signor Antonio bowed to Madam Scrooby but addressed himself to the squire.

"Sir," he said in the gentlest possible voice. "A thousand apologies for this commotion. It was entirely the fault of my little kitten, who was startled by the gunshot. I have presented myself as an humble applicant for the post of tutor to your daughter."

As Prudence said afterwards, nobody could make a nicer bow than Signor Antonio. Startled as she was, Madam Scrooby smiled. Pansy, glancing at the tiger and the demolished Leghorn, thought how small the tiger seemed when he was called a tiger but how large when he was described as a kitten. Remarkable as this riddle was, it was not more remarkable than Signor Antonio's transformation into a schoolmaster.

# CHAPTER 8

*In which Pansy and Prudence are intro-
duced to the Muses and make progress in
the application of the fine arts.*

R. SCROOBY was, as he said, quite taken aback at being so suddenly presented with a tutor. Nor did he feel Pansy's and Prudence's enthusiasm for this particular one to be any recommendation. He behaved for a while as though he believed that the less the girls liked the candidate the more satisfactory he would be. On the other hand since there was no other candidate, nor was there likely to be one, the squire felt loath to lose the only fish in the net even though he was a foreigner.

"Our own ancestors were foreigners here, sir, at one time," observed Madam Scrooby. "I daresay we may expect more and more of them as time goes on."

"I have no doubt that you are correct, madam," said Mr. Scrooby. "Though *our* ancestors cannot be described as foreigners — they were English. However it might be wise to try the man. Prudence certainly acquired nothing but ill temper with Miss Edwards. She is an estimable woman but I feel she did not quite understand our Prudence."

"Prudence is a deep one," said Madam Scrooby. "And she has taken a great fancy to Mr. Antonio."

"I wish she might learn to respect him," said Mr. Scrooby, "but beggars can't be choosers. He is the first schoolmaster to offer and we have been looking for three months."

While this conversation was carried on in the parlor Signor Antonio was sitting on the kitchen settle, drinking cider and giving Pansy, Prudence, Tryphena and Hagar the story of his life. They had never before been treated to such a story and Hagar came near to scorching her pudding as he talked.

He had been born in Venice, where the streets were rivers and the people went about their business in boats.

"My father," said Signor Antonio, "was a great prince of the church, Cardinal Esposito. I was brought up in the strictest possible manner and nothing that wealth could supply was denied me. Also nothing could exceed the grandeur of the palace in which I first saw the light of day. I was, however, spoiled and discontented. The children of the rich often are."

"That is so," agreed Prudence.

"So I ungratefully ran away from my virtuous parent at the age of three. My worthy father cast me off and I supported myself, first as a marionette and later as a performing bear. The world of the theater is not a wholesome atmosphere for a young person but at least I gained an education in the arts. My experience as a bear also trained me in the management of wild animals."

"I am acquainted with wild animals," said Pansy. "I ran away to live with the impala."

"Young people should not indulge in flights of fancy," said Signor Antonio primly. "Young people, young ladies in particular, should address their minds to facts and not give rein to romantic notions. I undertook to capture and make a study of exotic beasts, such as the camelopard and the gryphon. A gypsy with whom I formed an acquaintance made me familiar with this art. During the course of my studies in natural history I took the opportunity to perfect myself as a painter and a musician. I might have remained forever with my gypsy friends save for a disagreement which occurred between myself and a member of the civil guard in a town called Cremona where I was forced into temporary retirement. When I emerged from a period of abstinence and contemplation I decided to try my luck in the New World, and now good fortune has led me to this hospitable kitchen. For this I can never sufficiently thank the saints. I believe they have me under special protection. They shed their blessings where one least looks for them. Who would have thought to see such pastries, as you are now baking, my good woman, in the untrammeled wilderness of North America!"

"I'm sure you're welcome to one as soon as they're done," said Hagar, looking pleased. "But how is it that you haven't got yourself a wife? A fine fellow like you!"

"The felicities of marriage have so far eluded me," said Signor Antonio. "Ah, how I envy Squire Scrooby his peaceful fireside! What is more agreeable than the society of an accomplished woman! I hope, Miss Prudence, that you and your friend intend to grow up accomplished."

"Pansy will be accomplished," said Prudence. "I'm not sure about me."

"Shouldn't you like to sing Italian arias while accompanying yourself on the spinet?" asked Signor Antonio.

"I daresay. What are Italian arias?"

"If you have a spinet I shall be happy to enlighten your

ignorance," said Signor Antonio, "by performing one for you."

"The spinet is in the parlor," said Pansy. "Oh, please perform one for us. Master dotes on music. He will love to hear you." She took his hand and almost pulled him from the settle. "Afterwards you shall have some tarts, but please sing."

Squire and Madam Scrooby were a little startled by the sudden offer of a concert before they had made up their minds as to whether they wished to hire the schoolmaster or not, but out of consideration for Pansy's eagerness for music they composed themselves to listen.

The artist unlocked the spinet, dusted the bench and seated himself at the instrument. He held his hands like two drooping lilies over the keys for a moment. Then, as though plunging his hands in the music, he began to play and to sing.

*"Sento nel cuore,"* sang Signor Antonio, *"un certo dolore, la mia pace turbandola."*

Pansy had heard music in church. She had heard the faraway music of Africa, the faint ringing of the shepherd's kalimba — but never before anything like this. The music of Africa was lost with her babyhood, and the sound of psalms intoned through Mr. Stiles's nose was as the braying of asses to this. She sat rigid on her customary footstool at Mr. Scrooby's feet and her great dark eyes fairly bolted from their sockets. The singing made her long to sing too. She yielded to the longing and sang with him.

"Come along," said Signor Antonio. "That is right. Higher, faster." Pansy sang higher and faster. The parlor was full of music. Signor Antonio came to the end of the

song and dropped his long, blue-veined hands on his knees.

"I could teach you the real *bel canto,*" he said. "You have a perfect ear. Come to me. You are better standing erect. Never sit down to sing."

He ignored everyone but Pansy and her voice. He had become direct and rather sharp and seemed to have forgotten all about the story of his life, his dinner, his tiger and whether or not Mr. Scrooby wished to employ him.

"But aren't you going to paint our portraits?" asked Prudence. "You promised us some portraits."

"To be sure. Certainly. I shall paint your portraits. I shall become your drawing master, your dancing master and your music master. I shall teach you mathematics and the use of the globes. I shall undertake to improve you to the extent that not even your family will recognize you when I have finished with you. That is the aim of education."

"I trust that education also refines the moral perceptions," said Mr. Scrooby.

"I shall never neglect her morals, sir," said Signor Antonio. "But music provides an excellent grounding in morality."

"How so?" enquired Mr. Scrooby.

"We are told on the best authority that all angels are musicians, are we not, sir? It seems to follow then — if the number of musicians around the Divine throne is to be kept in good supply — that all musicians go to Heaven. It must follow from this that all musicians are people of the highest character. Otherwise they would not go to Heaven, but since they all do, we can only bow to the mysterious Providence which decrees that musicians are without exception heirs to salvation."

"You are ingenious, sir," said Mr. Scrooby a little sternly.

"Indeed, I trust so, sir," replied Signor Antonio. He returned to the spinet, reseated himself and played, singing the while in melting tones, "Angels Ever Bright and Fair." He gave a most delightful concert, concluding the evening with a song called "To Anacreon in Heaven" which swooped all over the scale and reached so high a note at one point that Prudence could barely squeak it although Pansy set up a splendid shriek and held it with a tremolo.

Although Mr. Scrooby refused to give positive assent to the employment of Signor Antonio on that evening, neither did he refuse him the post. He was torn between a natural distrust of strangers and the charm of this particular stranger's accomplishments. He stated that he would deliberate on the matter. In the meantime Signor Antonio might remain for a few days at the farm.

"At any rate," said Prudence, "you can paint our portraits to pass the time."

The next morning Signor Antonio arose early, a fact which Mr. Scrooby noted with silent approval, and fed his tiger. Pansy and Prudence assisted him in bringing the tiger a dish of milk and raw eggs which it devoured with no signs of gratitude. When the tiger had breakfasted Signor Antonio went to work on his picture. He took an easel from his pack and set it up in the flower garden. He fetched a chair and draped it in a swatch of purple velvet which he also took from his pack. Then he fetched the tiger and tied it on a short lead to a rosebush standard. He requested Pansy and Prudence to stand on each side of the chair and then he started to paint the picture. He sketched rapidly with chalk on a plain wooden board for about an hour and when he had made a satisfactory drawing he began to paint. He painted all morning. From time to time Tryphena or Hagar or one of the men would stop work to observe the progress of the painting and they stood before the easel aghast with admiration. Such a painting had not been seen before in the whole colony of Connecticut.

In the center of the painting sat Madam Scrooby. Signor Antonio explained that the splendid creature in a purple robe and wearing a crown of flowers was Madam Scrooby — somewhat idealized and treated in an allegorical manner. She wore a lace fichu over the purple robe and Signor Antonio devoted a great deal of care to showing the fine filigree of the white lace against the purple background of the dress.

"Mamma has no dress as fine as that," said Prudence. "She would have to send to Paris for such a frock."

"I told you that I was treating your mamma allegorically," said Signor Antonio, painting away. "I have painted many ladies wearing this dress. It creates an impression of grandeur." He went on to paint a great sheaf of golden corn in her arms. He put Pansy in one corner of the picture and Prudence in the other. Between them and at Madam Scrooby's feet he painted the tiger, very large. He painted Pansy wearing a leopard skin and a crown of something which looked rather like the bananas which she had eaten in East Africa. He painted Prudence in a white frock, wearing a crown of pink cauliflowers.

"You young ladies represent the continents of Africa and Europe," explained the painter.

Hanging in the air just over Madam Scrooby's head was the house. It had to be painted rather small in order to make room for a full-length portrait of Mr. Scrooby, who stood beside Madam Scrooby, wearing his blue satin coat and armed with a sword which also had emerged from Signor Antonio's pack. He was balanced on the opposite side by the arms of the Republic, surmounted by an eagle. In the rest of the available space were all the farm animals, the cows, pigs, horses, Mop, two cats and a chicken. They all stared straight out of the picture with great round eyes fringed with long eyelashes, painted in a most lifelike manner, like the lace.

"It is an excellent painting," said Signor Antonio, "one of my best."

Peter came up from the fields to get a measure of corn for his noonday meal and Signor Antonio painted him in as the continent of North America. The painting was already so crowded that the continent of North America had to be painted rather small but, as Signor Antonio said, it was important that it should be included. Peter was splendidly dressed in a warbonnet and he carried an axe.

"A tomahawk," said Signor Antonio. "It is necessary that he carry a tomahawk so that he will be recognizable as North America."

At noon Signor Antonio stopped for refreshments. Hagar gave him eggs, beans, pancakes and apple pie. He also drank a half gallon of cider. Then he composed himself to sleep for half an hour.

Upon awakening he looked primly at Pansy and Prudence and said, "We shall now have an hour of music. Your attention, please, young ladies. We shall address ourselves to the art of fingering."

He walked purposefully into the parlor. The room was vacant at this hour since Squire Scrooby usually occupied the study in the early afternoon, and Signor Antonio took possession of the spinet. His fingers rippled up and down the keys and he explained the principles of fingering. Having explained for the better part of a half an hour, he then put Pansy at the spinet and ordered her to put the principles into practice. Her little thin dark fingers could barely stretch eight notes but she copied his manner as well as she could. She had listened very carefully to the principles but she could not play as he did. The spinet, even after ten minutes of concentrated effort on her part, refused to yield the music which she wished to hear. She struck her hands together and burst into tears.

"There, there, Miss Sophia," said Signor Antonio. "You will play one day so as to make others cry, but before they cry they must scream with pain at hearing you play scales."

That afternoon Pansy and Prudence learned to play scales. Later in the day he ordered them to walk with him in the meadows where he pointed out various flowers to them and required the girls to learn the Latin names of daisies, buttercups, cowslips and various meadow grasses.

"Botany is an essential part of a refined education," remarked Signor Antonio.

"Our prospect is certainly diligent," said Mr. Scrooby to Madam Scrooby that evening. "Prudence seems quite exhausted by her lessons."

"I wonder can all that Latin be good for her," said Madam Scrooby. "It was not thought necessary in my day — for girls, that is. It would do no harm to a boy."

"I have always held that the female mind is capable of absorbing the same knowledge as that of the male," said Mr. Scrooby. "Prudence is no different to other girls."

"No, sir. She is exactly like them. Pansy is of a more studious turn."

"Nothing begets learning like example," said Mr. Scrooby. "If they study together they should make rapid progress. I believe we must let the foreigner try his powers. He may succeed where Miss Edwards failed."

"As you please, Mr. Scrooby. I don't believe in any case that Miss Edwards even knows the Latin name for a daisy. She never mentioned it when I went to school to her."

# CHAPTER 9

*In which Sophia Scrooby is undone.*

IGNOR ANTONIO — or Master Anthony as he now styled himself — having succeeded in worming himself into the affections of the elder Scroobys in his role of a schoolmaster, very nearly succeeded in worming himself right out of Prudence's. Even Pansy found him harsh. He was determined to do his duty by the girls, he said. Did they suppose he would take food, lodging and thirty pounds a year in order to let his young ladies grow up in idleness? No, indeed. They practiced scales and when they fumbled he struck their knuckles with a small ivory ruler which stung like a wasp. He also instructed them in the Italian language so that when they came to sing Italian arias they might pronounce the words correctly. He taught them to walk balancing a book on their heads, and to dance stately minuets. The thirty pounds a year had such a disagreeable effect on his character that he also insisted on teaching them sums. Both Prudence and Pansy hated these, but Prudence took some comfort in discovering that Pansy was as bad at them as she was. Pansy hadn't a notion of what to do with three and a half pears and two and a half apples, while all that Prudence could think of was to put them in a pie. They added and subtracted and multiplied and divided and got their hands rulered again for wrong answers and were sent back to playing scales. Tryphena was scornful of this occupation.

"Fine useful women they will grow to be," she said. "I should like to know where all these fandangos are going to take them. Straight to perdition I fancy. Italian lessons indeed! What should Pansy Scrooby do with Italian lessons? And as for Miss Prue, she had best learn something of household management. Otherwise she'll never get a husband."

Madam Scrooby taught the girls household management. As she often remarked, she had been trying to teach them this difficult subject for years. She set them to sewing a patchwork quilt. They sewed in the early evenings when the sputtering tallow candles were lit, sitting each on her footstool while Master Anthony entertained the household with music.

Altogether the summer of '76 was a busy and a quiet one. There was little visiting. People were too much occupied with high prices and short rations, with fears that Sir William Howe would sack Philadelphia or that General Washington would lack gold to pay his troops, to spend time or money on entertainment.

On the Scrooby farm Hannibal planted turnips and set rabbit traps: meals became a rather long progression of rabbit stews with turnips. Prudence quarrelled with rabbit stew and pushed the turnips around her plate, sulking at such monotonous and unpalatable food. Pansy ate her turnips uncomplainingly but could not manage the rabbit. In her rambles about the farm she had several times come upon rabbits, kicking and struggling in Hannibal's snares, and she yielded to the temptation to release the prisoners.

They hopped away into the underbrush, wounded but free. She could not endure to see a creature in a trap. The sight brought to mind recollections she would rather have forgotten, the slave ship and the long days in the barracoon and the thought which she tried to avoid thinking and for the most part succeeded in avoiding: that she lived in a snare. Prudence was free but Pansy was a slave. When the trapped rabbit looked at her with eyes glazed with pain and terror Pansy, without a qualm of conscience for the garden or the dinner, sprung the trap. Hannibal said that the wariest rabbits he knew lived on the Scrooby farm. They were as clever as foxes or woodchucks at finding their way out of his snares.

Two or three times during the summer children from the outlying farms came through the woods and across the meadows to see the tiger who had been put to live in an unused hen yard. They also came to gape at Pansy and Prudence, who were so different from these wild children of the tobacco farmers from beyond the woods. They seemed to think that the girls were a pair of live dolls who could be pulled apart and made to squeak. They were fascinated by the lace-trimmed petticoats, the thin-soled slippers with silk ties, Pansy's scarlet sashes and ruffled caps, but most of all by Prudence's sprigged muslin Sunday frock with the lace panniers on the sides of the billowing skirt. On one occasion, tiring of the fashion show, they all played war together. The boys, who had come to tease the tiger, were the Continental Army and the girls were the British. The boys explained that they planned to win the war and that the girls must arrange to lose it. This scheme did not appeal to Prudence in the least. With Pansy and the other girls she broke into the cucumber boxes, and when the boys charged the girls replied with a volley of cucumbers. Prudence also flung a toad which had been sunning itself nearby and the boys retreated in confusion. The girls retreated later when Hannibal saw the state of his cucumber frames. He hailed them before Squire Scrooby; the farm children were banished and Pansy and Prudence were soundly rulered by Master Anthony. They went without their dinners — squirrel stew this time — and were required to learn by heart the fortieth chapter of the Book of Isaiah, beginning with "Comfort ye, comfort ye my people, saith your God." There was little comfort to be found in all this.

"Education is surely a gloomy thing," said Prudence. "I don't know how we endure it."

"Certainly some good must come of it in the end," replied Pansy. "I say nothing of reading. I have derived a great deal of good from books but I can see nothing in arithmetic. I have here in the primer eleven and a half peascods from which I must subtract four and two thirds peascods. How many peascods remain? I can see that scarcely any peascods remain — not enough to do me any good at all. I had rather be at the scales. Master Anthony says that if I practice scales long and hard enough I might perform before crowned heads one day. I should like above all things to see a crowned head. I shall have no need of peascods then, I fancy. I expect crowned heads never even heard of them."

She went to the spinet and seated herself at it, lifting her hands as Master Anthony did and coming down on the chord as though splashing into a pool.

"*Ombra mai fu,*" sang Pansy in a long thrilling wail. "Crowned heads would like that."

Prudence whistled an accompainment. Prudence had neither Pansy's voice nor her gift for the spinet but she could whistle magnificently.

"Whistling girls and crowing hens, never come to no good ends," said Tryphena. "Here you go idling your time away at the spinet when you might be helping to weed the corn patch. Hagar and I have not six hands apiece, you know. Well, girls will be girls, I suppose. You'll eat it fast enough."

Pansy had watched Peter plant the corn in long straight rows and she enjoyed the sight of it when it came up. She remembered her mother sowing seed in long straight rows too. Finally the corn did appear. First, little green shoots pricked through the ground and these grew into stalks with bright green leaves. They made her think of the moon over Africa and the days before she was Pansy Scrooby and had sat beside the herdboy wondering about other people. One day Pansy went into the cornfield where Peter was hoeing, and the corn was nearly as high as her shoulder and the tassels had appeared.

"Peter," said Pansy, "who brought the corn here?"

"Corn's always been here," said Peter. "My mother, her mother, all mothers always plant corn."

"My mother planted corn too," said Pansy. "That was the way it was where I came from. I remember now. I used to watch the corn grow."

"Indians planted corn first," said Peter rather sulkily.

But Pansy wasn't so sure. In the mornings now when she woke up she would look at the corn springing in the field outside her window. Then before anyone was up she would take a cup of water and run out to pour it to the sun. And the corn grew beautifully. The spears were green as fever trees, the tassels golden silk, and the ears when the husk was stripped from them were like clumps of pearls. There was just the right amount of sun and just the right amount of rain. Hannibal was forced to admit that in spite of the sinfulness of the times he had never seen a lovelier summer. Pansy took care that it should stay that way and poured her cup of water faithfully each morning.

"It's going to be a fine harvest," said Mr. Scrooby when he walked the farm with Hannibal and felt the corn with his fingers. "God knows we need it. The times press hard upon us."

"Pickaninny do it," said Peter.

"Pickaninny?" asked Mr. Scrooby.

"Just like my mother," said Peter. "Go out in the morning to make the corn grow. Pour water to the sun. My mother bury a fish with the seeds — one each row. Pickaninny got no fish — all the same the corn grow. God watch her."

In August it was time for the haying. After the haying the turnips were picked and put down in the root cellar. Reuben picked the cucumbers and the onions and Hagar put them in the pickle barrel. Hannibal killed one of his valuable pigs, smoked and salted it and made it into ham and bacon. Then Peter, Hannibal, Reuben, Prince and John harvested the corn. This was a busy time and everyone was put to work. Prudence, Pansy, Tryphena and Hagar helped to strip the husks from the ears and to store them for the winter. When the task was done Hagar cooked an unusually good dinner and everyone had corn fritters with maple syrup to eat.

The time had come in fact to make ready for winter. The countryside was making ready too. Goldenrod bloomed in the meadows and made Master Anthony sneeze violently. But as the landscape became every day more red and gold he stopped the lessons, brought out the easel and tried to paint it. It was a very difficult thing to do. The trees blazed among the blue spruces which looked almost the color of peacocks but the paints seemed strangely dull. The picture wouldn't come right.

"It's easy to paint people and houses," said Master Anthony "but this business of landscapes is altogether different." He wanted very much to get the picture just right but he never did.

The days grew brighter and colder as October came on and the leaves of every tree were like candle flames. The evenings were cold now and everyone sat close to the fire at tea. Pansy and Prudence, who had at last managed to learn her letters, read aloud or played and sang with the tutor.

"I must have Pansy out onto the boards," said the tutor. "Already she understands *bel canto*."

Pansy didn't pay much attention to this. She did not know that she understood *bel canto* — nor indeed what *bel canto* was. She just sang. She thought she always knew how music ought to sound. She was so sure that she sometimes argued with Master Anthony about how fast or how slow a song should be sung and whether the song should be happy or sad. She even knew — or thought she knew — where she ought to breathe.

"She has temperament," said Master Anthony. "She is an artist."

Nevertheless Pansy's temperament made him angry. Sometimes he smacked her hands with his ruler and called her a wicked little panther. But Pansy went on being sure she was right and sometimes Master Anthony admitted that she sang best when she sang her own way.

"I should so like to take her before an audience," he sighed. "Alas, we are fearfully far from good company here. If only I had her in New York! She would become quite the fashion. I should bill her along with my tiger as *La Belle Sauvage* — the Ethiopian Angel. In New York there are many persons of taste and she would be patronized. She could sing for General Howe and his staff. I understand that Mistress Murray keeps a salon and that General Howe is often to be found there."

"Isn't General Howe the enemy?" asked Prudence. "Wouldn't it be better if Pansy went and sang for General Washington?"

"General Washington is always so busy," said Master Anthony. "He has no time to attend to music. But General Howe has nothing to do but wait for orders which never come. He has all the time in the world."

This statement proved to be true. General Howe never seemed to feel that time mattered at all. Autumn turned into winter, General Washington moved southward, and the war went on while Prudence complained that nothing ever happened in New Haven except that the weather grew colder. Master Anthony worried about his tiger and made him some winter clothes.

The tiger looked extremely funny in them. He had a coat made of an old patchwork quilt. It buttoned up high around his neck and covered him warmly along his back. Tryphena had helped to make it for him. At first she had said that she wouldn't sew for a tiger, but when she saw how the tiger shivered in the frosty mornings she made him his winter clothes. She sewed him into them too — as though he were one of the farm children who were always sewn into their clothes during the winter months.

"We can take him out of them in May," she said. Early in December there was a snowfall and everyone was snowbound on the farm.

The Scrooby farm lay buried in snow until the middle of January when a thaw set in which brought little relief from the tedium of the war winter. A thief was hanged in Hamden for stealing a horse. Tryphena and Hagar went to the execution and returned home much inspired by the exhortation they had heard from the parson who had accompanied the criminal to the gallows' foot. Mr. Scrooby prayed for the man's soul that evening when the family were gathered for prayers.

Only a week later a man in West Haven was tarred and feathered for being a loyalist. The news caused Mr. Scrooby great anxiety.

"He is an honest farmer," exclaimed the squire. "Surely our country needs no such demonstrations of enthusiasm."

Prudence and Pansy suffered from chilblains and from the gloom which increasingly afflicted Mr. Scrooby.

"Surely it can't be the war which bothers Papa so," said Prudence. "We haven't ever seen a redcoat here. I'm sure I wish we would. Things are so dull here."

Things got even duller when Hannibal came to his master and asked for his freedom. He wished to go for a soldier, he said. The whole world was fighting for liberty. Why shouldn't he?

Mr. Scrooby gave his consent and made Hannibal a freedman. He could not in all conscience refuse, he explained to Madam Scrooby. At the best of times he was not happy about the institution of slavery. "Our enemies have abolished it," he said. "We can scarcely refuse freedom to Hannibal to fight in our own cause."

"Hannibal is the most valuable man on the place," said Madam Scrooby. "I daresay you are right in the eyes of God, sir, but you have lost five hundred dollars."

"I should never in any case contemplate selling any of my people," said Mr. Scrooby. "I had rather declare myself a bankrupt and bid them all flee."

"If you go bankrupt, sir, the matter will be out of your hands," said his wife. "The courts will sell them up. You had best give them all their freedom. Now that you mention it, I conceive that they might be in a situation of some danger. Pansy would be in a sad case if we were to be pauperized."

"Pansy will remain with us whether we are pauperized or no. I would no more sell her than I would sell Prudence."

He fell to brooding over the fire, his cheek on his hand. "Without Hannibal," he said, "I scarcely know how we can continue."

John and Prince were not militarily inclined, Reuben and Peter were too old to fight and so the farm limped through the spring. But it was no longer possible for the farm to produce all that the household needed and those things which were needed had to be bought at terrifying prices. Mr. Scrooby no longer spoke of crops. He talked of nothing but money. The day came when Master Anthony walked into the parlor and turned back his wages.

"I shall work for my keep. Never never shall I desert the young ladies. I am yours to command, sir, as long as I may serve you. Pansy will yet sing for his High Mightiness, the President of the Republic."

Mr. Scrooby embraced the tutor and praised his fidelity. Master Anthony dashed the tears from his eyes with the back of his hand and seated himself at the spinet and played "To Anacreon in Heaven" with great expression. "It is a splendid song," he remarked, "and hardly anyone can sing it. It ought to be the national anthem."

But matters did not mend as the days drew out. Pansy and Prudence took long walks in the open air with Mop, glad enough to escape the sad atmosphere in the house. Their rambles took them far afield, to Hamden and beyond, to the caves where the regicide judges, Whalley and Goffe, had hidden from the King's constables, and halfway up East Rock where the white lady of the mist lived. They never saw the white lady although they saw hawks and foxes and once a cougar. He appeared upon a ledge just at sunset, and his body arched like a hunter's bow across the disk of the setting sun as he leaped from the ledge into the underbrush.

Pansy was accustomed to taking a book with her on these rambles and she would read to Prudence when they rested to drink their ale and eat the bread and cheese which Hagar provided.

"The poets," said Pansy, "console themselves with the beauties of nature in times of sorrow and we should make it our earnest endeavor to do so too."

"Mercy me, Pansy!" shrieked Prudence. "What have you been reading? How dreadfully sour this cheese is! And nobody can brew ale the way Hannibal used to. What did he want to go and fight for? I'm sure we need him much more than General Washington does."

"He is a freedman now," said Pansy. "He is like the citizens of Rome."

"Bother Rome," said Prudence. "And bother this hateful war. I don't see why we should have a war. If we hadn't had a war Papa might have taken us to London this year. Now who knows when we shall see it? The beauties of nature are no consolation at all."

The girls had fewer lessons now. Since Master Anthony had refused his wages he spent much of his time in the countinghouse with Mr. Scrooby, going over papers and sighing like a hurricane while his pupils stole out-of-doors unregarded.

Mr. Scrooby was too concerned over the money he was losing, Madam Scrooby too anxious to console him, and Master Anthony too aghast at the actual figures which danced like demons of doom before his frightened eyes to enquire closely where Prudence and Pansy went on their walks. Often the girls knew no more than Mop, who usually accompanied them, but one afternoon they stole through the pasture gates and into the copse which gave onto a narrow road called Sin and Flesh Lane. They had in the past been strictly forbidden to wander in that direction and they were both, and had been for some time, curious to know exactly what went on there. It was a narrow road, scarcely more than a cart track, its banks overgrown with burdock and bullbriar. A few minutes' walk brought them to the door of a cabin. There were a number of Negro children playing about the door, ranging in age from a baby to a tall girl of about thirteen. They were dressed in rags, and Pansy and Prudence in their fine, warm cloaks stopped to stare at so much misery. Pansy had not seen such children since she had left the slave ship.

While this silent interchange was taking place a horse and wagon drew up to the door of the cabin, and from it stepped a man, a white man of the meanest sort. His clothing was shabby and filthy, his jaws unshaven and his manner rude and wild. He stood with his hands on his hips outside the cabin door and bawled, "Jen."

A stout Negro woman appeared at the door. She gave the man a curt nod and said, "Well, have you the money?"

"I've got the money if you've got the goods," said the man.

"Plenty of that where it came from," answered the woman. "Here you, Jenny. Master's come for you and for Jack and Bill, so look sharp. It's time you were off. I'll throw in George for two dollars if you've a mind to him. He's little but he's sharp for his age. He's worth the money."

The man surveyed the child who appeared to be George and shook his head. "Too small. I'll take him next year."

There was an exchange of money for children. No more than that. The man counted fourteen bills into Jen's hands and she laboriously counted them again, and when she had made sure of the fourteen she gave the tall girl a

shove, picked up the baby and disappeared into the cabin, while the man stowed the girl and two young boys into the wagon and drove off.

Pansy and Prudence were much mystified and stole home as though they had been witnesses to a crime.

They would have preferred to have let their visit to Sin and Flesh Lane remain unnoticed at home but curiosity overpowered their discretion. That evening they asked Tryphena who Jen was.

"Jen who?" asked Tryphena.

"Jen of Sin and Flesh Lane," said Prudence.

"What do you know of Sin and Flesh Lane?" demanded Tryphena wrathfully. "Who told you of her? Have you been running away there? You know you're forbidden to go there."

Since liars go to Hell when they die, Pansy and Prudence admitted that they had been there. Tryphena shook them both until their teeth rattled. "I should send you to Master for a good birching. Such wicked disobedient girls I've not seen."

"Papa doesn't believe in flogging for girls," said Prudence primly. "He says the philosophers don't recommend it. It isn't a modern method."

"The devil take modern methods!" exclaimed Tryphena. "We flogged girls in my day and they learned to mind their parents and nurses. Now listen to me. Jen's a witch and I don't know what all besides. She has children and *sells* them. She deals with every rogue in New England. That felon who was hanged — he ran errands for Jen for years before he came to the gallows. If I ever hear of you in Sin and Flesh Lane again I'll birch you myself. It's no supper for you tonight and to bed with both of you."

She shooed them upstairs and into the bedroom where she left them to ponder their evil ways for the rest of the afternoon. Pansy solaced their captivity by reading to Prudence out of a pretty little book about a wicked girl who had been struck by lightning for neglecting her religious duties.

Prudence found the story unpleasant. "I wish there was a story about a *good* girl who was gored by a mad bull," said Prudence, "or one about a bad girl with a rich uncle who gave her a great deal of money."

"I don't believe that there is such a book," said Pansy. "Such things don't happen in books. They happen only to real people. There is no sort of use in filling books with things that happen. They wouldn't be instructive and nobody would read them."

She went to the window and looked down on the driveway leading up to the front door. "There are some people come to call," she said. "There is a carriage at the door."

"Oh good," said Prudence. "Perhaps Tryphena will forget that we are to have no dinner. Let us go to the head of the stairs and see who has come."

The girls left the bedroom and peered down the stairwell. There were several men in the hall and with them Mr. and Madam Scrooby and Master Anthony. But these were not ordinary callers. They were shabby, angry-looking men and they had with them a roll of papers which Master Anthony was inspecting with very visible distress. Madam Scrooby was weeping and embracing her husband, seeming to try to comfort him for some very great distress.

"There is nothing that we can do," the girls heard Mr. Scrooby say. "We must sell up, madam. We are nothing but common debtors without a penny to bless ourselves with. This house belongs to the bailiffs, and you and I and Prudence to the four winds. Anthony, I thank you for your good service but I can no longer offer you even a roof. We are completely undone."

"And Pansy, sir, what is to become of Pansy?" the girls heard Madam Scrooby cry.

"Let me not think on Pansy," answered Mr. Scrooby and turning, groped his way into the study. "Pansy too is undone."

# CHAPTER 10

*In which Pansy Scrooby is sold up with the household goods and pursues her adventures amid scenes quite other than those to which she has hitherto been accustomed.*

SQUIRE SCROOBY was bankrupt. His investments had failed, his farm was worthless to him without the labor to work it, and he had no means left in the world. The war had destroyed him although no soldier had come near his house. But the bailiffs came, as they came to many others in those days, and took the furniture and the carpets. They even took the clothes and the cooking pots, the silver, the spinet and the pictures. Squire Scrooby stood before the window of the parlor looking straight ahead of him with his blind eyes while everything that he had ever owned or cared for was swept away by angry, discourteous intruders who behaved as though he and all his household were no more than sheep to be sold at market.

Prudence screamed at parting with her frocks and playthings, and Pansy cowered in her closet with a growing dread, saying nothing.

"They are taking all our nice things!" wailed Prudence. "How shall we dress ourselves and eat? Mamma says we are to go to her relations in Canada but how shall we manage in Canada with no clothes?"

Pansy shook her head.

"You don't seem to care," said Prudence accusingly. "Canada won't be a bit like home."

"They can't take me to Canada," said Pansy bitterly. "I could manage in Canada with no more than what Jen's children wear. But I am not to go. I am to be sold. I have heard Tryphena and Hagar speak of it. We are all to be sold."

"It isn't true!" gasped Prudence. "Papa and Mamma would never sell you."

"They do not wish to sell me," replied Pansy. "But they cannot help it. They must because Master has fallen into debt. He is ruined."

"I won't let them sell you. I shan't let them take you away!" screamed Prudence. She jumped wildly to her feet. "Papa, Papa —" She was tumbling down the stairs with Pansy after her. "You aren't going to sell Pansy?" Her father, hearing her, looked up from where he sat in a cane chair near the empty fireplace. He looked like an old man. He seemed shrunk into himself and even a little bewildered.

"They are taking Pansy away," he said. "I can do nothing. I had meant to tell her. I could not." He turned his white eyes to the blank hearth.

Pansy walked into the parlor and stood staring at him for a moment. Prudence was hanging on his shoulder, sobbing and protesting.

"They will come for our people this afternoon," said Squire Scrooby. "There is no hope."

"And what is to become of Master Anthony?" cried Prudence. "And why can't he help us? We helped him once."

"He must help himself now," said Mr. Scrooby. "He is clever. He will find employment. As for us, we must lay our bones among our Canadian friends. Your mother's people will help us — to all save honor. As for Pansy, I dare not think on her."

He had not known that Pansy was in the room and he spoke in such utter despair that Pansy for a moment forgot herself.

"Sir," she cried. "Do not despond! All is not lost. I shall never be parted from you for long. God will not allow it."

"I did not know that you were here, my child," said the squire. "I cannot speak for God. His ways are beyond my knowing. I only know that we must lose you."

"I shall come back to you," said Pansy. "I shall find a way."

Squire Scrooby bowed his head. "You have more faith than I do, my child. And the fault lies with me. Had I freed you when Hannibal went to war, when Master Anthony advised me, you might have been journeying to Canada with us now. You are on my conscience forever. They will take you today and I cannot stop them."

"I will come back," said Pansy.

The slave dealers who had bought the Scrooby people from the receivers came that afternoon for Pansy, Tryphena, Hagar, John, Prince and Reuben. Peter, who had never been a slave, packed a bundle and vanished silently into the woods without any leave-taking.

Those last moments in the Scrooby household reminded Pansy of the last hours in her village. Although everyone knew that danger was everywhere, the arrival of the receivers seemed to astound both the Scroobys and their unfortunate servants to an equal degree. The receivers and their clients had a bad time of it. They had not only Squire Scrooby's attitude of outrage and contempt to meet but the angry disbelief and finally the hysterical rebellion of Prudence, who clung to Pansy until the last, moaning and lamenting until one of the men who had come to fetch her away lost his temper, and snatching his purchase by the upper arm sought to place her in the wagon in order to bear her off.

It had not occured to Pansy that anyone, no matter how evil his purposes, would seek to lay hands on her. And she recognized this man who touched her now as the same ugly fellow — with weak, red-rimmed eyes and fingernails bitten to the quick — who had bought the three children from Jen of Sin and Flesh Lane. His hair grew down over his temples concealing his ears. As he stooped to catch Pansy up around the waist she was aware of his face very close to hers and the sight of a scar. He was crop-eared — a criminal of some sort.

"Unhand me, sir," cried Pansy. "Set me down at once!"

The crop-eared man stared for a moment at Pansy and then with a laugh he fetched her a blow across the face which made her gasp but did not stop her struggles. Prudence was more rapid in her reaction than Pansy. She sprang at the man like a hound upon some lumbering beast and sank her teeth in his wrist. The man gave a cry of pain and anger and sent Prudence sprawling.

"That for you, you Tory cub. You'll leave me and my blacks alone or I'll slit your tongue an' you were any loyalist mare."

With Pansy squawking in his arms he hurried out of the house and pitched her into a wagon which was hitched to the post at the front door. But even then her farewells were not said. As the man was whipping up his horse Master Anthony darted down the front steps. He engaged in a frantic and pleading conversation. Pansy was almost certain that she heard him make an offer for her and that the crop-eared man angrily refused it. The wagon pulled away from the house. Through the front windows of the parlor, curtainless now and looking strangely blind, like Squire Scrooby, she could see her foster father looking out the window with his white eyes. Pansy waved but of course he could not see her. Prudence was raging in her mother's arms. Madam Scrooby was in fact forcibly holding her within doors. The wagon turned the corner of the driveway and the house vanished behind its rampart of trees. The horse trotted out onto the main turnpike and the man headed the wagon southward.

The wagon had gone some little distance when Pansy heard the sound of a horse behind her and, turning, saw a rider galloping toward them down the road. Within a few minutes she perceived that it was Master Anthony. He was riding swiftly and came abreast of the wagon quite quickly.

"Pansy!" he cried. "Pansy!" He slowed his horse to a trot and came alongside the wagon. "Tryphena, all of you — Master Scrooby is for Canada. Do not forget. Canada. Pansy — remember — you will yet sing for his High Mightiness and for all the serene highnesses and holinesses in Europe. Pansy, I shall find you yet. I shall follow you."

"You'll follow her to the gallows," growled the crop-eared man. He struck out at Master Anthony with his whip and the horse shied violently, nearly unseating his rider.

"Be off or I'll have the constables on you for interfering with an honest man's business."

"Honest!" exclaimed Master Anthony. "An honest man who trades in human flesh! Tell me, my honest fellow, how came you by that scar along the temple? I thought that only counterfeiters lost their ears in these enlightened times — hardly honest tradesmen."

The slave driver replied to this remark with a savage slash of his whip. "Off with you, mountebank, or I'll see you in the stocks before morning and have you charged with spying for loyalists besides. I'll have my slaves to market and the likes of you won't stop me." He glared over his shoulder into the wagon and the unhappy prisoners cowered under the upraised whip. The driver hastened the horse with a dexterous flick of the whip on the animal's eyelid, and Master Anthony called out, "Take this, Pansy. Here are some things of yours." He tossed her an embroidered bag, closed at the mouth with a drawstring. In it were Pansy's Bible, her sampler and wool to work it with, a change of linen and a little purse containing a shilling and a sixpence. Clutching her belongings, Pansy cried out, "Thank you," to him as he sadly turned his own horse back toward the farm. The wagon wound its way along the turnpike toward the town of New Haven.

The captives sat uncomfortably and in dejected silence. Smart, swift-tongued Tryphena and the rollicking Hagar were crushed into silence; they were mute as the prisoners whom Pansy had encountered at the barracoon in Moçambique. Both of them clung fixedly to the bundles which they had brought with them and stared ahead of them with dull, angry eyes. The three men, John, Prince and Reuben, who all wore fetters, sat with bowed heads, and John wept. As though in answer to the dark mood of the travelers a thin rain began to fall, and the driver draped himself in a canvas while his charges were allowed to become drenched. After about an hour of slow jogging the wagon reached New Haven, turned into the main square, and made its way toward the gaol, a long, squat building which gave rather pleasantly onto New Haven Green. Here the prisoners were decanted into two cells, the women with Pansy in one, the men in another, and left with a meager ration of bread and sour beer for the night.

In all Pansy's travels she thought that she had never spent so cruel a night. She would have preferred the slave ship any day. The gaol not only served as a debtor's prison and as gateway to the stocks and the gibbet but also as a madhouse, as Tryphena and Hagar informed Pansy. The cold, mournful hush of the prison was frequently broken by strange, wild laughter, by snatches of tuneless singing and by an occasional wail, which must have come from a human throat for no animal could have made so weird a sound. At twilight there had been a further diversion as the students and professors of Yale College, hard by the gaol, collected for evening prayer in chapel and added their psalm-singing to the cries of lunatics and the oaths of the thieves and vagabonds, who cursed freely and violently at the solemn procession in its black gowns wending its way to the chapel. Pansy tried to say her prayers but could not address her thoughts to them in the darkness, the stench and the noise. She stopped praying and began to think.

Her condition was pitiable but not, in her view, as pitiable as that of the Scroobys. What was to become of them? Who would play with Prue and who, above all, would sit with Squire Scrooby and read to him, now that Pansy was gone? Where was Canada and how did one get there? Pansy's mind was so much occupied with these considerations that she ceased to think about herself and began to concentrate fiercely on a plan of escape. The fact that she was in the hands of a crop-eared man had made a profound impression on her mind. What was it that Master Anthony had said? Counterfeiting — that was the word for his crime, an unfamiliar word but obviously charged with meaning for the slave driver.

"Tryphena," whispered Pansy, "what is counterfeiting?"

"There you go with questions again," said Tryphena. "It's a crime, that's what it is."

"But what kind of a crime?"

"Making false money. What difference does it make?"

"Is that why he is crop-eared?"

"I didn't see that he was. But I reckon 'tis so if he's cropped. He has a gallows complexion if ever I saw one. We'll be lucky to escape with our lives. You keep a civil tongue in your head or he'll whip you. You're mighty unfortunate, now that I think on you. Master and Mistress did you no service to bring you up as they did. You'll never live through what's before you."

With these comforting words Tryphena laid her head along her arms and composed herself for what rest she might get. Pansy crept close to her and slept uneasily too.

She had never been particularly fond of Tryphena, but the thought that tomorrow might bring worse companions than Tryphena and her scolding prompted her to cling to her.

In the morning the crop-eared man threw open the doors of the women's cell with the announcement that he had company for them. Three more persons were admitted to their circle. These were a tall girl of thirteen years or so and two children, little boys of seven or eight. Pansy looked at them first with indifference but after a second glance she found something familiar in their appearance. They were the three children whose mother had sold them on that dark March day a few weeks previously.

"At least," thought Pansy, "my family did not willingly sell me — I am infinitely more fortunate than these poor people. Tryphena is wrong. The Scroobys did me no disservice."

The trio whom the crop-eared man had shoved into the cell huddled wretchedly together in one forlorn heap. Nobody had the heart to greet them and they seemed content to maintain a grim silence. Presently the

crop-eared man brought bread and distributed it. There was hardly enough to stay the stomach of one, but the morsel was carefully divided into six equal shares. The prisoners passed the morning in silence, broken by the whimpering of the smallest of the boys and an occasional sigh fetched by Hagar from the depths of her heavy frame.

Towards midday — Pansy reckoned it was midday by the slant of the sunlight on the damp wall of the cell — the heavy door swung open on its creaking hinges and disclosed not only the crop-eared man but another individual, who stepped into the cell, cutting quite a figure, at least in Pansy's eyes.

He was a dwarfish, elderly man, tricked out in a wardrobe of which every article appeared to have once belonged to a different owner. His coat was green and too large for him. The trousers were purple and in spite of his small size, too short. He wore a neckcloth so old that it had turned yellow, and patches of it were gray with dirt. He wore a yellow satin waistcoat which had once been fine but was now badly torn and streaked with food stains. Mice appeared to have made off with most of the wig which surmounted his features. He wore slippers with tarnished silver buckles. But the most startling detail of his appearance was a scar on his cheek, which his pitiful attempts at a beard seemed more to emphasize than to conceal.

He was such a comical figure, and so unlooked for, that Pansy gave a crow of laughter that surprised even herself. Her laugh pealed out in the darkness of the cell and seemed to give both Crop-ear (as Pansy had nicknamed him in her thoughts) and the scarecrow with the scar a bad start.

"What is there to laugh at?" demanded the scarecrow. "You've no business to laugh. If you go on like that you shall be flogged. Where did you get those clothes? That is an expensive cloak. The fur is the true weasel. Give it to me." He put out his hand and took a snatch at Pansy's cloak.

"My master, Squire Scrooby, gives me my clothes," returned Pansy haughtily. "Do not touch this cloak. It is my master's. You shall not have it," she hissed.

"I'll have the cloak," said the scarecrow, "and that fichu too. That's real lace — French. I've seen lots of it. And a coral necklace too. I'll have the coral necklace. You belong to me."

"You paid for me, not my clothes and jewels. They do not belong to you. You shall not have my necklace. Don't you dare to touch it. You are nothing but a common thief."

The man gave Pansy a long look of disbelieving malice.

"So we have a lawyer among us. I'll have you flogged for that until you cannot stand. How dare you call me a thief?"

"Because you are stealing my clothes and my jewels. Because you have a brand on your cheek. Anyone can see that you are a thief. A man was hanged in Hamden only a few weeks past for stealing a horse worth fifteen shillings. My necklace is worth much more than that. And it is not yours. They will hang you up outside of New Haven Gaol — this very gaol — if you steal my necklace."

The man made a queer strangled sound in his throat and fetched Pansy a box on the ear.

"You stop that talk. I know nothing of hangings. Give me the necklace of your own free will or I'll find a way to make you. And you are nothing but a slave and can own nothing. The necklace belongs to me. I'll have it if I kill you for it."

"Careful of that kind of talk, Jonsey," said Crop-ear — he appeared to be rather amused by the battle. "The slave trade ain't what it used to be. I heard as how they hanged a gentleman in Jamaica for killing of his slave. You and the young lady here better not disagree too far or she'll have you before the magistrate and strung up before you know it."

The scarecrow, sensing that he was being baited, rounded on Crop-ear. "You're encouraging her to be saucy. Where did you find this piece of work? Did you buy it honest? If you didn't I'll have you up as a receiver of stolen goods and they'll get your other ear off you."

They were glaring at each other and Pansy, seeing them quarrel, sensed an advantage. She moved toward them, shaking one sharp little finger.

"You will be hanged!" she cried. "Both of you! They will take you to the Green and hang you up in front of the church and I shall come to see them do it. I shan't mind a bit. It will be just like the Newgate Calendar. And when you have hanged God will send you straight to the eternal fire and the worm that dieth not. You will swing in God's hands like a spider over the abyss of Hell and he will dash you into the flames with no more care than you would dash an insect. You are damned — you are not of the Elect. You are vessels of wrath!"

Jonsey and Crop-ear were actually retreating before her. The other prisoners stood watching as birds watch a serpent.

"She's a witch!" squeaked Jonsey. "That's no picka-ninny. It's a witch. It ought to be burned."

"You're afraid of me," hissed Pansy.

For answer the crop-eared man caught her by the upper arm, dragged her from the cell, down a corridor and into a small chamber. Here he threw open the door of a cup-board and into it he thrust Pansy, slamming the door to with a bang that shook the gaol. Pansy screamed and beat the door with her fists — but in vain.

"That for witches," Pansy heard Crop-ear say. "You're a superstitious fool, Jonsey. She's been bred high and taught to talk fancy. Tory family, I should think. We'll sell her south and get her out of the way. Be quiet, pickaninny, or I'll cut your tongue out."

Their voices died away as they left the room and Pansy heard no more. She beat once more upon the door and screamed, but there was no answer. She was all alone in the dark with no help near her.

# CHAPTER 11

*In which Pansy is transported to new and unfamiliar scenes and finds friends in adversity.*

ANSY'S KNUCKLES were sore from pounding against the cupboard door, she had toppled her cap from her head, her skirts were twisted, the ribbon which tied her cloak was choking her, her left slipper was untied, and one of her stockings had come loose from its garter. She felt about in the darkness until she found her cap and set it straight on her head. She fastened her stocking, smoothed her skirts, tied her slipper ribbon about her ankle and settled down in the darkness to think.

It was of course pitch-dark in the cupboard and poor Pansy got very little consolation from her brains. She first considered the question of how much money Crop-ear had paid the bailiffs for her. A great deal more money than she could ever come by, she imagined. Even supposing that she found a means of earning money, it would take years to save enough to get her to Canada. If she had three pounds, how long would it take her to gain thirty — which was what Master Anthony had earned at the Scroobys? And perhaps it would take much more than that to buy a horse to get to Canada on. The horse which the thief had stolen was worth fifteen shillings — was it a good horse? Would a fifteen-shilling horse go as far as Canada? Pansy wished she had paid more attention to sums and the use of the globes.

Where was Canada? And where did Crop-ear and Scare-crow propose to take her? Slaves were often taken to New York to be sold, she recalled. Mr. Scrooby had spoken of it and had mentioned that New York was a great port. Pansy had felt profoundly indifferent to New York in those days. She had bestowed no thoughts on it at all. Now it began to be of burning interest if only as a place to escape from. Or perhaps she was not to be taken to New York at all but merely sold as a field hand or servant to a local farmer, persons whom she, as Sophia Scrooby of Squire Scrooby's Acres, had scarcely taken notice of since her arrival in Connecticut.

The thought of serving some harsh Yankee farmer or his sharp-spoken wife with her rough clothes and crude country speech made proud Pansy cringe. They would call her Scrooby's wench and seek to bring her pride down. Pansy fingered the true weasel at her collar and felt her pride well in her throat. The blood rushed to her cheeks at the thought that Crop-ear had laid his hands on her, had soiled her smooth skin and beautiful clothes with his filthy paws and had put his scarred face near to hers. She was his prisoner — she, Sophia Cecilia Scrooby — but she would not remain so long. She had marched across Africa, she had survived the Middle Passage, she had taught herself to read, she could play the spinet and sing Italian arias, she could embroider and dance a minuet as neatly as any girl on two continents. She could even read a little Latin. She would not remain the prisoner of a counterfeiter and a receiver of stolen goods.

"I shall think," said Pansy to herself, "and I shall pray. God will hear me. He will be proud of me for thinking."

These resolutions had scarcely crossed her lips — she had uttered the words aloud — when the door of the cupboard opened and she saw Jonsey, the scarecrow, framed against the light.

"You can come out now, pickaninny," he said, "but you must be civil or you'll get nothing to eat."

Without deigning to answer, Pansy stepped out. Jonsey took her by the arm and led her back to the cell. In it were the three children, but Hagar and Tryphena were gone. He thrust Pansy within, turned the key in the lock and disappeared.

Pansy looked about her. "Where are the others?" she asked.

The big girl shrugged. "Gone," she answered. Pansy felt that this reply was unnecessarily brief but since the girl did not look inclined for conversation she refrained from comment. Jonsey returned with food after a few moments had passed, and again asked Pansy if she intended to be civil.

"I am not in the least hungry," replied Pansy. "You may keep your food."

"You've a haughty devil in you," said Jonsey, "but there was never a devil yet that could hold out against no food at all. Here you, Jen. Since she won't eat there's all the more for you."

It was clear to Pansy that for some reason Jonsey was wary of her. Perhaps he really believed that she was a witch. She would do everything she could to reinforce him in this view although now that she thought about it she was uncertain as to how witches behaved — apart from calling up the devil, a very wicked thing to do. She recollected that Mr. Scrooby had cast doubt on the existence of witches — yet there was certainly a witch in the Bible. Even Mr. Scrooby had not denied the witch of Endor.

Jonsey left some bread and ale with Jen and disappeared. The big girl divided it out into four portions and gave one to Pansy. "You'd better eat," she said.

"No, thank you," replied Pansy. "I feel no inclination for food."

Now that Jonsey was gone Jen unlocked her lips. "You had better eat whether you will or no," she said. "What good do you do yourself going hungry? You've a long road ahead of you. No good dying of hunger on the way."

Pansy fingered a piece of stale, sour bread. "Do you know where they are taking us? Do you know what has become of Hagar and Tryphena?"

"They was sold yesterday, after Master Jonsey locked you up. Some men came for them and took them away. They say they'll take us to New York and sell us to the slavers on the great river. Nobody wants children here. He couldn't sell us in Hamden nor yet upriver in Hartford. I heard Jonsey say all about it. There's a ship from foreign parts laying to in New York. She's not part of the fighting. The foreigners will exchange us for sugar and rum and take us to the swamp country."

"The swamp country!" exclaimed Pansy. "But where is it?"

"I don't know," replied Jen, "but it's a long way off."

"But I can't go there," declared Pansy indignantly. "I must escape. I must go to Canada."

Jenny gave a contemptuous snort. "I reckon we'll all go where they say. And you'd best not sass Master Jonsey or he'll flog you."

"He daren't," said Pansy. "He dare not touch me."

"Don't be a fool," replied Jenny. "He'd as soon kill you as look at you. I'm right sorry for you, I am. You've been raised that soft. I'll do all I can to take care of you, but if you give Jonsey trouble I can't help you and likely you'll get us into trouble too. Jonsey's a mean one. Mammy told me so before she sold me."

"Yes," said Pansy wonderingly, "your mother sold you. I remember now."

"She sold my big brother last year," said Jenny. "She can't feed us nohow. She feeds the young ones on what she makes and sells us as we come along. That way we all get to eat. I sure hope there's more feeding down in the swamp country than up here. You go ahead and eat your share of that food. It ain't much but it's better than nothing." She eyed the portion hungrily as she spoke.

Pansy looked at the older girl in some astonishment. She was a big, clumsy, homely girl but it was clear that she had a benevolent nature. She might have kept all the food for herself and her brothers but she had divided the portion with absolute fairness.

"You are very kind," said Pansy. "I did not intend to be ungrateful. I thank you with all my heart." And she took her portion of bread and ale and made a meal.

"I hear tell," said Jenny, "that there's great farms down in the swamp country and they'll sell us to work on them. But they say they'll sell you in the town because you wouldn't be no good to a farm."

"But what town is it?" asked Pansy.

"A Spanish town," said Jen. "That's what Master Jonsey says it is. I don't rightly know what Spanish is but down there they speak right funny so you can't understand what they say. And there's pirates there and witches."

"Spanish people are . . . Spanish people," said Pansy hesitantly, trying to think what she knew of Spanish people. She had learned a pretty song once about a Spanish lady who had wooed an Englishmen. Master Anthony had barely mentioned the Spanish people when instructing her in the use of the globes. Truly she had made but scant use of her opportunities for gaining useful information.

Jenny was looking at her dolefully. "Master Jonsey thinks you're a witch. Most likely he aims to sell you to another witch."

"I am not a witch," said Pansy. "Only wicked girls are witches. I am a good Christian. I was baptized in New Haven Church. Squire and Madam Scrooby are my godparents."

"Well then, mebbe they'll sell you to a pirate."

"God forbid," said Pansy firmly. But her heart sank within her. Jenny lapsed into silence. As evening drew on the cell grew chilly and Jenny took the littlest of the two boys, Bill, in her arms and chafed his little feet. Pansy drew Jack close to her, and in warming him somewhat warmed herself. The child slept in her arms, his dark, curly head lolled on her shoulder.

Crouching in the darkness of the cell Pansy prayed, fixing her thoughts on the righteous and vengeful God of the Israelites. On this gloomy night she took some comfort in the thought of his wrath. He would smite her enemies and confound her ill-users. When she had been restored to her friends, Pansy decided, she would address herself to forgiving the bailiffs, the creditors, Crop-ear and Jonsey, as a good Christian maiden should, but it was too soon to think of forgiving them that night. She prayed fervently for the destruction of all slavers, and if God chose to damn them — well, that was no affair of hers. She would let God run his own business for once and not interfere with teasing him to save people who took children away from their homes and who probably wouldn't appreciate salvation anyway.

The constantly recurring thoughts of the alternative of a witch for a mistress or a pirate for a master chased sleep from her eyes and Pansy brooded for most of the night on how to evade such a fate. Perhaps if she clung closely to Jenny it would seem that she was part of one family and would be sold together with her new friend and the boys.

"Oh, Jenny, don't leave me," breathed Pansy into the darkness, and Jenny half woke.

"What you moaning about?" she said sleepily.

"We must keep together," said Pansy. "I won't be sold to a witch or a pirate."

Jenny reached out a hand and patted Pansy on the knee. "Ain't nothing you can do about it, honey," she said and went back to sleep.

The night wore away at last. There were rustlings and stirrings in the gaol. Someone dropped a heavy vessel full of liquid and there was a crash, a splash, followed by a concert of oaths. A mad prisoner bellowed for his servants and dressed down the gaoler who came to try to silence him. The bells of Yale Chapel chimed sweetly and the sound of students at prayer floated through the barred windows of the gaol. Jack and Bill woke up and began to cry with hunger and cold. Pansy rose to her feet and smoothed her skirts. Jonsey appeared at the cell door and squeaked for the prisoners to show themselves.

"Now," he said surveying his wares through the bars, "we're off to New York, that's what. I've brought you a breakfast and you'd best get on with it for there isn't much time. With any luck we'll be in New York by tomorrow night and I'm handing you over to Pedro Alvarez. He'll take you to New Orleans. I've no mind to saddle myself with a bunch of children, although mind you, I like children and I've a tender heart. Look how well I feed you. I'm a patient man and I spoil children but Pedro Alvarez — he's different. He won't stand for no airs and graces, and if you don't mind your ways you'll find he'll feed you to the sharks and that would be a pity for you'd miss seeing New Orleans and they say it's a fine town. If you behave yourselves and don't make him no trouble it's likely he'll sell you all to a kind man with a big white house and you'll eat chicken all your lives. But if you give trouble — there's French pirates and voodoo women. They eat pickaninnies like you. So mind your manners."

He opened the cell door and placed a meal of bean porridge, bread and ale on the floor and disappeared.

The little boys fell upon the food like animals but Pansy and Jenny looked at each other aghast. Even Jenny was horrified to hear her story confirmed and Pansy was momentarily in despair.

"We shall be devoured — if not by sharks, then by witches. We shall fall into the clutches of pirates — the worst of men." She turned with the resolution of the drowning on Jenny. "We must stay together. There must be some means — together we can care for one another."

"I don't see what's to stop a witch-woman from eating us all," said Jenny. "What's the use in staying together?"

"We can be servants to the gentleman with the great farm. Anything is better than to be eaten."

"They'll eat us if they've a mind to," said Jenny, and proceeded to make a breakfast. She swallowed a considerable amount of bean porridge and then turned to Pansy, her wits apparently somewhat sharpened by food.

"I aim to stick with you," she said, "and I think I see how to do it. I'm going to play the fool. I can't talk, see. I can't do nothing, withouten you tell me to. But once you tell me I can do anything you want. That way they'll leave me with you and we can take care of each other."

"And what about the boys?" asked Pansy, glancing at them. They did not look as though they would make much of a meal but there might be no accounting for the tastes of the monsters which they were all about to encounter.

"I'll think of something," said Jenny. "Eat your breakfast. You get slow-witted iffen you go hungry."

Pansy swallowed a little porridge. It was vile food and although she was hungry she would have had to be much hungrier to tolerate such stuff. Jonsey came to the cell and called "Here you, Jen."

Jenny did not answer. Pansy twitched her skirts daintily above her ankles and picked her way into the middle of the cell where she stood primly in a shaft of sunlight, her hands folded in front of her. Jenny stood dumb and sullen.

She looked like an idiot. Her lazy stance and lusterless eye seemed to strike Jonsey amiss.

"You Jen, why don't you talk? They told me you were a clever wench when I bought you."

"She does not understand you," said Pansy. "You may tell me what you wish and I shall convey it to her."

"You!" said Jonsey. He drew back a little. "What's come over you? Have you put a spell on her? Take it off. Make her talk."

Pansy saw that he was still afraid of her. Perhaps this was, after all, what being a witch meant. People became afraid. The thought gave her courage.

"Jenny!" she said imperiously. "Jenny, come forward." Jenny slouched to the door of the cell.

Jonsey stepped back yet another pace and called over his shoulder, "Silas! Yoo-hoo, Silas!"

He was answered by a snarl and the sound of someone stamping his feet into a pair of boots in some nearby room. Silas, whoever he was, was evidently putting on clothes. Jonsey did not appear to have removed his. Untidy as he had looked last night he was even more so this morning.

"I don't know what kind of a lot you've brought me," complained Jonsey loudly. "One's raised up so fine that she'll never do for a servant. I told you last night she was a witch. The big girl's a natural. She can hardly speak — and the other two aren't more than babies. Here you," he turned savagely on Jenny. "Can't you talk? Are you a fool now?"

Jenny hung her head, plucked at her ragged apron and turned in her toes. Under her eyelashes Pansy could see that she was the picture of the village idiot.

"See what I told you," said Jonsey. "Soft-headed. She won't fetch a shilling. This whole business has been more trouble than it's worth. And I'm worried about the fancy one."

Silas now swaggered into the room buttoning his waist-coat. He turned out to be Crop-ear. He surveyed the four children with a sour expression. "It was all I could find," he said. "Folks aren't selling their people. You know that as well as I do. Some of them have got their freedom and gone for soldiers. Labor's too short now for anyone to part with a good slave. I could have got you a couple of dotards in their nineties if you'd have liked that better."

Jonsey evidently decided to console himself with philosophy. "What's done is done," he said. "We must get what we can and make the best of it — though it's enough to make a man turn to another trade, I declare. What's the good of going to all this trouble, I should like to know, if folks won't make it worthwhile."

"What trade had you in mind?" asked Crop-ear. He took a gulp from a jug of ale which he held in his hand. "Phew, this is very, very vile ale."

"There's smuggling," said Jonsey. "With the British out there will be room for smuggling. No more of these shocking penalties."

"No government will allow *that* trade," said Crop-ear. "You'll be as bad off under the Yankees as under the British. There's no help for the poor, I always say. Might as well stick to your blacks and hope they don't decide to free them all."

"Whoever heard of such an idea?" said Jonsey.

"Oh, there's talk of it," replied Crop-ear. "Tarring and

feathering for such loose-tongued wretches, I say. The Sons of Liberty will deal with them!"

"It won't happen," said Jonsey comfortably. "It's against nature. It's time to get on the road, Silas. Bring the cart around and let us be off."

Crop-ear lurched out of view and Jonsey began to fuss over his charges. Pansy had kept herself presentable but Jenny and the little boys were a sorry sight. Jenny in particular, goggle-eyed and openmouthed, seemed to defy all hopes of becoming reasonable merchandise. Her forlorn and stupid appearance taxed all of Jonsey's ingenuity. He even produced a clean apron for her and a mobcap with which to cover her cropped head. When he had done with her she looked like some madman's idea of a chambermaid perhaps, but not one that any sane person would ever take into his household.

"You will have to do," sighed Jonsey. "Can you speak at all? Do you understand what I am saying?" Jenny sniggered but made no reply.

"Just as I thought," said Jonsey. "A natural. Well, hold your tongue. The quieter you keep the better, I suppose. As for you," he turned to Pansy, "what's happened to all your fine talk?"

Pansy again glanced at Jenny to see if there were any sign of life but Jenny was still looking stubbornly at the ground.

Jonsey herded the children out the door and into the street and from there into the little wagon in which they had traveled the day before. Crop-ear and Jonsey mounted a rickety bench which served as a box from which to drive the horse and the wagon set off toward the New York pike.

Pansy's miserable journey to New York occupied two days. There were occasional brief stops for food and rest but the slavers were in a hurry and spared neither themselves nor their horse. In some ways the two days seemed as long to Pansy as her trip through the Middle Passage. She was more frightened now than she had been then and more painfully aware of what was happening to her. She was also angrier than she had ever been. The flesh seemed to wither on her bones whenever the slave dealers approached her to lift her to and from the cart and she threw such glances of hatred and fury at them that once or twice they recoiled from her in fear as though she had been a live coal.

On the evening of the second day the highway along which the cart was traveling gave way to cobblestones; houses replaced the trees and hedges; and a variety of smells attacked the travelers like a swarm of gnats.

There were people everywhere, soldiers, sailors, beggars, fishmongers, blacksmiths, tanners in their reeking aprons, butchers' boys selling high-smelling meat and bakers carrying trays full of buns which Jack and Bill sniffed appreciatively.

Jonsey noticed the sniffing and remarked that they had better content themselves with enjoying the fragrance, since he was not buying fresh buns for pickaninnies. "They say there's a rebel army camped across the river" he complained to Silas. "What if they attack? The British will murder us all in our beds."

"You'll soon be out of here," said Crop-ear, "and safe in a rebel gaol for trading with the Spaniard against regulations. Don't look so frightened, Jonsey. What's a brand or two on the cheek to a bold, lusty fellow like you? Why don't you turn pirate and work the south coast down toward New Orleans? They say there's rare freight to be found in those waters. Pedro Alvarez will die a rich man."

"At a rope's end," said Jonsey. "Pirating's not for me. I never did like the sea. I was always seasick at the sight of a sail. No, I'll stick to dry land. Besides you shouldn't talk so loud. Little pitchers have big ears."

"You mean that cargo in the wagon," laughed Crop-ear.

"The Scrooby wench. I don't like her looks. The sooner I'm rid of her the better. I don't aim to go pirating." He turned and glowered at Pansy. "You hear that, wench? I'm no pirate."

Pansy, who had taken out her Bible and was reading it with studied attention, treated him to one of her glances. He gave a snarl and faced forward on the box.

"Hurry that horse, Silas. We should be at the wharf by now. I'll trade this lot for a cask of rum. You'll see if I don't."

## CHAPTER 12

*In which Pansy Scrooby makes a sea voyage*
*and a new and useful acquaintance.*

HE DAYS grew warmer and the sea bluer. The *Hermosa* was having an uneventful journey down the coastal waters of North America. The flag of Spain, fluttering from her mast, allowed her to pass undeterred through American waters. She ignored the war and pursued a southerly course, floating on the water as leisurely as a gull.

Rather to Pansy's surprise she found that she, Jenny, and the boys were the only human cargo aboard. Captain Alvarez was, it seemed, indifferent to cargo. He kept a few chickens and a goat; he took on a small load of tobacco at

150

Charleston; but otherwise the ship appeared to have no object in view. Pansy knew that he had traded with Jonsey for her. Jonsey, glad to be quit of his own bad bargain, had settled for a keg of spirits and some rusty firearms. Pansy and Jenny wondered aloud and often what Alvarez wanted with them. He was a somber bearded man with a heavy squint. He was not cruel or taunting as the slavers had been. He rarely spoke save to give orders and his men were like him. They were filthy and to Pansy's sensitive nose they stank like corpses.

Once Pansy plucked up courage and asked him what he meant to do with her and her friends. He answered in his heavy Spanish accent that Jack and Bill would make good cabin boys and that he would find a use for the girls somewhere.

The answer brought Pansy and Jenny little comfort but Alvarez would give no other. The captain busied himself with his charts on the bridge and the crew kept sullenly to the care of the ship. A strict watch was kept on the horizon. The children were free to roam about the ship and were fed with the crew. This idleness did not please Pansy but Jenny and the boys seemed to find it restful.

Grateful for her sampler and her Bible, Pansy knitted her brow over her future and stitched her embroidery. The ship sailed on into waters which grew ever bluer as the sun grew warmer. Sometimes Pansy wondered if the ship were bound for Africa — and if for some reason she and her friends were to return to those shores. Was it possible that Pedro Alvarez meant to make a missionary of her? It seemed doubtful. She could see herself as a missionary, and even possibly Jenny could be prevailed upon to convert the heathen, but clearly the boys were intended for other careers. In any case she could not imagine them as missionaries. They were far too naughty. She speculated on the matter with Jenny.

"If they are taking us to Africa there will be nothing to do but to become missionaries and convert the heathen," said Pansy. "You should learn to read."

"Oh, dear," said Jenny. "I don't believe I could."

"Nonsense," said Pansy. "I taught myself. I'm sure I could teach you. And it would be a diversion. Do but try. See, here is the first chapter of Genesis. It isn't really difficult. If Prudence could do it, you could. All it says is that in the beginning everything was void and without form and that God created the world and then he made man. He made all the animals too. Was that not clever! Let me read it to you."

She read the story of the Creation and threw in the Flood for good measure. Jack and Bill stopped rolling about on the deck and crept closer to hear it. They all agreed that it was a most interesting story but only Jenny felt equal to trying to read it to herself.

"Don't worry about Jack and Bill," she said. "If they are sailors they won't have time for reading. I'd better do it by myself."

She labored over the letters in Pansy's sampler and then, as Pansy had done, learned to write them out, using the deck for a slate and a piece of charred wood for a pencil. She made good progress, being naturally quick, and shortly wrote her name and the names of the first five books of the Bible. Pedro Alvarez occasionally watched her working with Pansy and chuckled loudly that Jonsey was well and truly cheated. He had sold the girl for an idiot — and Alvarez had got two little witches for a keg of bad rum and some guns that wouldn't shoot.

Pansy and Jenny were engaged in reading and writing one afternoon when they observed that the ship's crew had suddenly plunged into activity of a kind it had not shown since the *Hermosa* had left the port of New York. All the bustle sprang up because the watch had suddenly let out a shout from the crow's nest. Pedro Alvarez appeared on the bridge and issued a volley of orders. The ship's flag was run down and another flag appeared on her mast. It was black with a white device but Pansy and Jenny could not quite make out what it was. The captain ordered every stitch of sail on and the ship, gathering speed, began to rush the waves like a horse rushing at a gate.

Looking about her at the open sea Pansy could spy no reason for all this excitement, until finally it occurred to her to glance at the watch and to follow the line of his spyglass. He had fixed on a point on the horizon, and by straining her eyes Pansy could see a speck in the far distance which, while she watched it, resolved itself into the shape of a vessel. The *Hermosa* was pursuing this ship like a hound after a hare and gained on her every moment. The other ship was struggling to get away but as the *Hermosa* drew nearer it was clear that the quarry had not a chance against the swift Spaniard. She was weighted down with cargo, a squat merchant vessel going about her business, while the *Hermosa* carried nothing but her crew and cut through the water like scissors through silk.

The chase lasted for about two hours. The sun lay just below the merchantman's topsail as the *Hermosa* came alongside. Then while Pansy and Jenny looked at each other aghast, the crew tore the air with a war cry and at the same time there was the sound of cannon fire. The merchant ship's mainsail burst into flame and there was an answering volley from her guns. One of the Spanish sailors fell to the deck.

"Pirates!" shrieked Pansy. "We are a pirate ship!" There was more gunfire. Catching up her Bible and her embroidery, Pansy siezed Bill, who happened to be nearest to her, and rolled under the longboat slung against the port rail. Jenny, with Jack, followed her. The Spanish pirates were swarming to the rail and through the smoke and confusion Pansy could see that they were boarding the merchantman, which was rolling helplessly now, with her masts broken and her sails burning on her decks.

Neither Pansy nor Jenny could have told afterwards how long the battle between the two ships lasted — but they knew it must have taken several hours. The sun seemed to burn itself out in smoke and noise. All that the children could see when they finally crept from the shelter of the longboat was a burning mass some hundred yards off, a few stars through the veil of smoke, and the dark forms of the pirate crew returning from the wreck — carrying the spoils of this adventure to the ship's hold. This task was carried out with great dispatch. The *Hermosa* did not linger near the scene of her crime. Abandoning her smoldering victim, she struck her ensign, put about, and flew before the wind, as though this time she had some definite destination and wished to reach it quickly.

"Oh, the poor people," wailed Pansy. "Not one left."

She hid her face in her hands to shut out the sight of the burning ship.

"Where do you think we are going?" whispered Jenny, trembling. "Oh, I wish I might have been sold on some plantation. I never thought to come to pirates. Sure, they'll hang us all if they catch us. I've heard they always hang pirates."

"They can't hang us," said Pansy firmly. "We are not pirates. Oh, if only we could rescue someone!"

"I'm hungry," wailed Jack suddenly from his corner. Jenny began to rock on her heels and said she wished she were dead.

"I'm hungry, I'm hungry," cried Bill, catching the idea from Jack.

"Be quiet," said Pansy. "Be quiet. Pirates are the wickedest of all men. They might kill you if you cry." She rose and smoothed her skirts. "I shall find you something to eat. And if there are any prisoners I shall bring them something too. We must not stop here all night being frightened. We must think how to outwit these pirates."

"I'm hungry," repeated both boys at once. "I'm *hungry*."

"That's all they ever say," said Jenny.

"Keep them quiet until I return," said Pansy. "I shall try to find food for them."

She left the group under the longboat and crept forward until she came to the hatch which led to the crew's quarters. She could hear the pirates below shouting and laughing. The ship was noisy tonight, celebrating a successful catch. The smell of spirits, mingling with the gunpowder smell, warned Pansy that the pirates were probably in no mood for catering to other people's appetites. She crept away from the hatch and sidled forward for some distance, holding on to the rail. Here the noise was fainter and Pansy stopped, looking about her for a light to show where the hatch leading to the galley lay. Her eyes encountered a shape in the shadows. She crept closer to inspect it and found herself staring up into the face of a man. He was lashed to the mainmast and stood there patiently in his bonds, returning her gaze.

"Oh, sir," breathed Pansy.

The figure at the mast gave a slight start. "You speak English!" he said.

"Yes, sir," replied Pansy. "I speak only English — and a little Latin."

"English will do for our purposes," returned the man. "Have the goodness, if you please, to untie me. These cords cut me abominably."

"At once, sir. I shall untie you at once." Pansy found the cords, and a few minutes of picking at the knots released the stranger, who gave himself a shake and stepped away from the mast. In the darkness Pansy could gain only a very indistinct impression of his appearance but he seemed to be young — he had a young voice. Pansy could also discern white neck linen and the gleam of silver shoe buckles. He turned to Pansy and made a slight bow.

"Your servant, ma'am," he said. "I am profoundly grateful. Captain John Forsyth, at your service. To whom am I indebted for the valuable service which you have just rendered me?"

"Sophia Scrooby, sir," replied Pansy, and curtsied.

"Ah, Miss Scrooby — I presume you are Miss — from

your stature you appear to be a lady in early youth. An enchanting time of life, fraught with promise, bright with the bloom of young womanhood. The name of Scrooby is honored in its bearer. But who, may I ask — or rather what — are you? Indebted as I am to you for your distinguished notice, I also confess myself puzzled as to how you come to be here at this time in the shape, shall I say, of a deliverer. This is a pirate vessel. I am what is usually described as booty. I trust you do not occupy the same unhappy position. If so let me offer my condolences. At the moment I have nothing else to offer."

"I am a prisoner too, sir," replied Pansy.

"I grieve to hear it. Are they holding you for ransom? I trust your relatives may come down handsomely and soon. Any hopes I may have had for making my fortune in the New World by buying a plantation in New Spain are dashed for the moment — or until such time as my affectionate relatives feel equal to meeting the demands of my captors. But you have come like a good fairy and released me from my bonds. Your manner of speech suggests that you are not a stranger to the pleasures of learning. May I inquire as to your origins? Where, in short, do you hail from, and whither were you bound when you had the sad fortune to be captured?"

"I am a slave girl, sir," replied Pansy. "I was sold."

The captain bent down and looked closely at Pansy. "God bless my soul! So you are. Allow me to say, Miss Scrooby, that you astound me. Nay, I am horrified. Well, at that rate one might even say that your fortunes might be considered on the mend. What shocking fellows these colonials are!"

"Oh, dear me!" cried Pansy. "It was all against Squire Scrooby's will. He would not have sold me. But he became a debtor. The slavers fetched me away. And I was not always a slave. I intend to be free again and then I shall rescue Mr. Scrooby and Madam and Prue and we shall all be happy again."

"Miss Scrooby, your tones would move a stone to tears. You should be on the stage. You are quite worthy of the pen of the author of *The Castle of Otranto* — a very pretty romance, ma'am — but may I suggest that we find a more propitious spot in which you may recount your story to me. Further, if you are sufficiently familiar with this hulk to find me some form of sustenance, I believe that food would help to restore my spirits and to compose my mind. Then perhaps we might consider how best to confront our situation."

"I was looking for food when I came upon you, sir. The pirates are eating and drinking below. They have forgotten all about my friend Jenny and the two little boys. But if you will wait I shall try to steal into the galley and find food for all of us."

"Admirable child!" exclaimed the captain. "We shall share and share alike. Clearly you have a heart of gold."

Pansy withdrew and made her way to the galley. A faint light from its depths showed her that the premises were deserted and in great disorder. She laid hold of a handful of biscuits and a jug of something that might or not have been drinkable and took her prize aloft. She went round the starboard side of the ship where she left food with Jenny and the boys, and then found the captain again. He was extremely grateful. The biscuits were not full of maggots, as might have been expected, and the jug contained rum, which, as the prisoner said, was highly medicinal and warded off all manner of fevers and agues.

"We must lay our heads together," said Captain Forsyth, "since we find ourselves companions in this time of doubt and danger, fire, shipwreck and war. You are a young lady of courage and resource. I am a gentleman, whose qualities in this regard are not, I trust, inferior to your own. It is possible that we may devise some scheme for putting an end to our captivity and restoring our former fortunes. Pray tell me in more detail what your former fortunes were and how it was that you fell into the hands of these pirates, not one of whom will remain unhung when I have found the means of deliverance from their hands. It is possible that one of your former friends, hearing of your plight, just might assist you. If they were as kind as you say, surely hearing of your fate they would make every sacrifice to help you to a better destiny than that of handmaid to a pirate captain."

"Oh, sir," said Pansy tearfully, "you do not understand. Their case is worse than mine. They have nothing to sacrifice. And my master is a blind man. He cannot help me. It is I who must find and help him."

"My good Miss Scrooby," said the captain, "if it stands so badly with you, then there is no more to say. I see that we are comrades in misery and since we having nothing else to rely upon, we must make use of wit and courage alone to help us to a better state. Come, do not cry. Let us make ourselves as comfortable as possible under the longboat. In my opinion we shall remain undisturbed for some time to come since you say our captors are making holiday below and are probably dead drunk to a man at this moment. You shall tell me your whole history and together we shall devise the manner of our escape. Before you begin upon a tale which promises to be agreeably protracted, let me ask if you have any notion where the next port of call of this vessel lies."

Pansy shook her head. "No, I have no idea of it."

"When we were boarded," said the captain, "we were one day's journey from the Spanish port of New Orleans. It is my guess that our captor, being by his speech a Spaniard, purposes to put in there. The coast is, as I understand, infested with these brigands and he may intend a reunion with others of his profession in some concealed inlet of this mysterious shore."

"I think it very likely, sir," said Pansy.

"Let us therefore beguile the time until daylight with a mutual exchange of confidences and a discussion of plans. You befriended me tonight, ma'am, and I assure you that a Forsyth never forgets a favor. To this estimable quality our family owes its survival from the deplorable times of the Commonwealth to the present. It will be my earnest endeavor to assist you to happier circumstances, and I trust that you will undertake to render to me such services as will from time to time suggest themselves to you, and which may well lead to our escape. You will benefit me and I shall preserve you. You have earned the right to style yourself Sophia Scrooby preserved, and to quarter your arms not only with the Jolly Roger which flutters from the mainmast of this vesssel but also with an African lionet — which on account of your courage and decision of mind you have every right to assume — rampant."

Without very well understanding this speech, Pansy crept with her new friend under the longboat and, as he said, beguiled the hours of the night with all that had befallen her over the past years, including the battle with the Impi and her life with the impala, the slave ship and her education at the hands of the Scrooby family. By the time she had told her tale the sun had come up, and she and the captain could discern in the warm morning mist a thin green ribbon of land in the distance.

"I believe," said Captain Forsyth, "that we are sighting the port of New Orleans. Heigh-ho."

## CHAPTER 13

*In which Pansy encounters Madam Melanie and other inhabitants of the fens of Louisiana and takes counsel upon how to mend her fortunes.*

HE *HERMOSA* lay to all that day off the pale green coastline. After the adventures of the previous day the captain and his crew returned to the subdued routine which they had held to during the voyage down the coast. Nothing was said when the English prisoner was found to have been released from his bonds. He was conducted below decks with a slight show of courtesy and he shared the hold with Pansy and her companions while the crew went about its business.

It was ragingly hot in the hold. Jenny stripped the shirts off Jack and Bill. The two children fretted with the heat and the girls tried to raise a wind with their aprons, but to very little purpose. After many hours two crewmen appeared and signed to Captain Forsyth that he was to accompany them aloft. He went and returned within an hour.

"I have been the recipient of a great deal of Spanish courtesy," he said when the hatch closed again above his head. "Captain Alvarez informs me that I have nothing to dread but the slow passage of time. Letters requiring my ransom money will be dispatched to my relatives in London. I shall remain a captive here until the money is received. Nothing could be simpler. All that I need is patience. I reckon that with any luck I may receive word from my fond uncle that since I am not worth a tittle of the three thousand pounds at which the pirates have been pleased to value me, he will pay a quarter of the price — capital and interest to be laid at my charge on my release. My uncle and the pirates will bargain amicably until such time as my uncle sees fit to quit this vale of tears — and the old villain is remarkably healthy save for a touch of the gout — or until Pedro Alvarez may meet with foul play, one of the hazards of his profession. I assume that all of this may take twenty years. By that time I shall be forty-five. The heiress upon whom I have set my heart will have given her hand and fortune to another. My little inheritance will have fallen into the hands of my rapacious cousins, and I shall emerge from these toils a wretched, aged pauper with a suit at law which will occupy my declining years — assuming I am to be allowed any declining years. It won't do."

"I should think not indeed, sir," said Pansy. "Surely your uncle —"

"My respected uncle would far rather part with twenty nephews than with one shilling. The pirates on the other hand, being simple fellows with an inordinately high opinion of the state of family affections in England, have assured me that nothing will force them to deliver me but the payment of three thousand pounds — and they have assured me that they intend to inform my uncle that failure to meet their requirements will result in damaged goods. They promise to spoil my beauty for me —"

"That would be a shocking pity!" interrupted Pansy.

"I thank you and I agree. You have exquisite taste, I see.

I wish your wits might be as sharp as your address would lead me to suppose. Escape, Miss Scrooby, is essential."

"Indeed, sir, I am sure nobody wishes to escape more than Jenny and I do. We shall surely devise some means —"

Captain Forsyth looked at her pensively. "If what you have told me of your life and adventures is true — and I see no reason to disbelieve you — I think you to be both cunning and bold. Besides that — though I fancy I am not a superstitious man — I think you may be lucky. Captain Alvarez speaks devilishly poor English but enough to make me understand that he intends to disembark by night and conceal his ship in one of the inlets of this coast. He seems to maintain his own harbor and some sort of residence in the swamplands here. Escape from this vessel at this time is clearly impossible, but we may be more fortunate once ashore."

Captain Forsyth's words proved correct. At nightfall he and the four children were taken ashore by the pirates. The darkness combined with the swamp mist was so heavy that it was impossible for anyone to see anything of the route which they traveled. The longboat delivered them to a little dock stretching out into the water and the captain and two members of the crew came with them. The pirates took the precaution of tying up Captain Forsyth very tightly and for good measure lashed him to the rail of the wagon in which they traveled.

The journey inland took the better part of a cloudy night, and when dawn came and the captives were able to see for themselves the landscape through which they traveled — at a snail's pace, for the horse between the wagon shafts was old and the footing uncertain — their spirits did not rise. Pansy had never imagined such a desolate country. Gaunt trees, from whose boughs hung streamers of moss like torn webbing, covered the landscape. The party seemed to travel through an interminable swamp. The horse was sometimes ankle-deep in mud and a warm, evil mist lay everywhere. The wagon wound through thickets of thick, coarse leaves and stunted trees, and across narrow man-made causeways with the swamp water lapping at the wheels. Watching from her place in the wagon Pansy saw a familiar object lying motionless along a rock.

"Look," she whispered to the captain. "Do you see him? The shadow?"

He looked and nodded. For once words failed him. He looked a little sick. Long and low and wicked the alligator crouched on its stone, quiet as a corpse. It stared at the people in the wagon with lidless eyes and one of the pirates made a gesture, doubling up his two middle fingers and pointing the index and little fingers at the beast.

"He makes the sign against the evil eye," said Captain Forsyth.

Captain Alvarez ventured a rare remark in English, pointing to the alligator.

"You are not good," he said, addressing Pansy, or so she thought, "I throw you to him."

Captain Forsyth pursed his lips. "I fancy he means what he says, Miss Scrooby. I do not find him full of scruples."

Pansy made no answer. The wagon pursued its course, penetrating ever deeper into the thicket. At one stage the travelers reached a wide body of water, and here the wagon was loaded onto a barge which after an hour's poling attained the opposite shore, to the great relief of the pirates' victims. The water was full of alligators, their leathery backs glinting in the first light of morning.

About an hour after dawn the wagon track seemed to widen to something like a road lined with trees. Presently the wagon traveled over a causeway and a long, squat house, built of logs and standing on low stilts, revealed itself. The wagon came to a stop and Pedro Alvarez put his fingers to his mouth and let out a shrill whistle. The door of the cabin opened and a huge woman appeared in the doorway. She was immensely tall, black, and brilliantly dressed in a crimson gown with a yellow turban on her head. She came running toward the wagon uttering shouts of welcome, and as she came near Pansy could see that her dark face was made dazzling by a pair of huge, pale, blue eyes.

Her good mood changed to anger when she saw the cargo which Alvarez had brought. Pansy could not understand Spanish, but the woman's tone made it clear that she was disappointed in what she saw. For a brief while Pansy wondered unhappily if the whole party were not to be thrown to the alligators, but after some argument which ended with Alvarez's suddenly shouting several angry sentences at the woman, she ceased her railing, and turning to Pansy said, abruptly and in English, "You may get down and come into the house. And mind your manners or I shall give you much trouble."

Her look was as ferocious as her words. Pansy, followed by Jenny and the boys, entered the cabin and the pirates assisted the English prisoner from the cart and brought

him indoors. They untied him and the woman brought food, a plate of something that looked and tasted strange and perhaps poisonous to Pansy's palate, but since the travelers had eaten nothing for many hours she made a meal of yams and observed to Captain Forsyth that they should no doubt thank God for what they had received.

"I trust I am not lacking in gratitude," sighed the captain, "but it seems a slender mercy."

While they ate, Pansy and her friends were at liberty to observe the other inmates of this compound or village or whatever it was. They were all Negroes, many of them children although there were a few young girls among them. The group seemed to consist of about fifteen people. Apparently they were all the servants or neighbors of Pedro Alvarez and they took pains to wait on him — he received a good deal more on his plate than yams. There was a pot of stringy meat simmering over a fire at one end of the cabin and he ate heartily of this, and also drank thirstily from a jug of spirits which the tall woman brought him. With each drink his temper seemed to improve. He finally gave a few commands and the newcomers also received a share from the pot. It was chicken cooked in spices and Captain Forsyth this time expressed sincere gratitude.

While they were eating Pansy noticed that the tall woman had retired to a place near the cooking pot and sat there toying with something which lay near the coals over which the pot simmered. Straining her eyes through the gloom of the cabin, she was at last able to see that it was a small snake which the woman caressed and even crooned to from time to time. The hair rose at the back of Pansy's neck. She nudged the English captain anxiously and he acknowledged the nudge with a grimace. He had seen the snake.

The meal over, the woman arose from her place by the fire and came over to Pansy and the captain. She stood over them hugely, smiling down in a curiously good-natured manner, her blue eyes flickering. After a few minutes she said to Pansy, who stood beside her friend, silent under the woman's steady smile, "Do you know who I am?"

"No, madam," replied Pansy. "I do not."

"Don't you wish to know?" asked the woman.

"I trust that my young friend is not deficient in natural curiosity," interposed Captain Forsyth, "and she will certainly have no objection if you choose to tell her."

"You have a marvelous ready tongue, sir," said the woman smartly. "See that it doesn't wound you — like my serpent here." She stretched out her arm and drew from under the sleeve of her robe a small snake, the one which she had fondled by the fire. Jenny, crouched nearby, gave a short scream and the two little boys drew in their breath. Pedro Alvarez and the two pirates across the room began to laugh. Pansy stood her ground and neither screamed nor moved. The woman, a shade less good-naturedly, said, "I shall tell you whether you like it or no. I am the queen of the dead. Do you know why you are brought here?"

"No, madam," said Pansy softly. She was very much frightened now but she wished not to show it.

"Are you not afraid?" said the woman.

"It will do me no good if I am," replied Pansy desperately.

"Well said, Miss Scrooby," exclaimed Captain Forsyth. "You speak the truth."

"You may call me Madam Melanie," said the woman. "Pedro tells me that he bought you cheap from a man in New York and that you are a witch's girl."

Pansy looked at her wonderingly. The woman was not joking. Nor did she wait for an answer. As Pansy was to learn in the weeks that followed, Madam Melanie never waited for answers. She never asked questions either but merely made flat statements. Those who wished to reply might do so but the replies made not the slightest difference to what Madam Melanie thought or did.

"Your master was afraid of you," pursued Madam Melanie. "You prophesied that he would be hanged. Tell me — what else can you prophesy?"

Pansy cast her eyes about the room. The scene with Jonsey rose in her memory and she recalled that he had been extremely frightened. Now she longed to prophesy that the good Lord would strike Madam Melanie and her friends the pirates dead with lightning but she hesitated. She remembered that Squire Scrooby had once told her that among the heathen it was a common practice to sacrifice the bearers of bad news to the gods and she suspected strongly that Madam Melanie was a heathen. Pansy stole a glance at Captain Forsyth and saw that he was looking at her intently but she could not guess what he wished her to say. She folded her hands in front of her and looked modestly at the ground.

"I cannot prophesy today," she lisped. "I am but a very little witch. I have learned only small things."

"Come," said the woman, "you are trying to cheat me.

Pedro says that you told your master his crime and that you are the cleverest witch seen in the north. Do not lie to me. I know a witch when I see one. Black girls do not wear such frocks and petticoats as you have, nor furred cloaks neither, nor such a fine coral as you have. They said that when your master tried to take it from you sparks flew from it, and the hand of the slaver turned to stone when he stretched it forth to strike you. Assuredly you are a witch and a powerful one. You need not lie to me. If you are good you will come to no harm. I shall show you how I rule the dead and Pedro will be your friend. Speak a spell to me. I shall show you one of mine in return."

Glancing about her Pansy looked for a way of playing for time. Her wits told her that it would serve her turn to agree to the part of a witch but she could not imagine how to play it.

"Show me a spell, Madam Melanie, and I shall show you one," she said cautiously.

Madam Melanie looked pleased with this reply. "I see you drive a bargain," she said in an approving tone. "You do not trust me. That is right. You have learned that in this manner we are often trapped and so undone. Very well, I shall show you some of the things I do." She went to the door of the cabin and called through the mist, "Josephine, Josephine."

A young girl came running and Madam Melanie gave a few directions in an undertone. She spoke in French and Pansy did not understand her. The girl disappeared in the swamp mist but returned shortly carrying a black cock. She crept into the room with the cock and placed it in the middle of the room. Madam Melanie fetched a small drum which stood near the fireplace and then came back and loomed over the cock. Then she crouched on her haunches and began to play the drum softly with her fingers and to chant as she did so, her head swaying on her long neck like some great tropical flower on its stalk. The cock crouched in the middle of the floor and did not move. The girl, Josephine, crouched near Madam Melanie and began to sway and chant too. From where she crouched in the corner, Jenny began to mark time with the drum. The whole room was filled with a strange thunder. Only Captain Forsyth and Pansy felt themselves separated from it and watched, captivated — but not enchanted. Higher and higher rose Madam Melanie's chant. Josephine began to wave her hands above her head and Jack and Bill began to stamp to the drum. In the midst of it all crouched the cock, motionless, his eyes glazed.

Madam Melanie gave the drum a final thud and kicked it aside. Josephine stopped swaying and Jenny and the boys fell silent.

"So do I govern the dead," said Madam Melanie. "Now I have shown you my spell show me yours."

Again Pansy glanced at the Captain and received no sign. She took a deep breath and opened her mouth and began to sing. She sang the "Ombra Mai Fu" from Mr. Handel's opera *Xerxes*. Master Anthony had once remarked that her singing of this aria made chills run up and down his spine and she only hoped it might have the same effect on Madam Melanie, to say nothing of the chicken who still crouched motionless on the floor.

She gave the air as much breath as her lungs could muster and sang it very strong and true. As she sang she observed that Captain Forsyth had risen from his seat and came nearer and nearer as she sang. With the final note he was at her side and he turned with a flourish to Madam Melanie.

"I advise you, ma'am, to exert the greatest care with this witch. Let me assure you that never in my life have I heard such powerful magic. And when one considers the age of this witch!" He made a gesture which suggested that he had witnessed a miracle.

Madam Melanie, who had at first come as near to looking bewildered as was possible to her, now turned to Captain Forsyth with an expression which almost resembled gratitude.

"So you are familiar with this magic. It seems to you strong. I have not been cheated. Pedro is right. The child is a witch."

"Indubitably."

"But what will this magic do? We have heard a spell but nothing is changed."

"Madam, is it possible that you do not observe the changes which have occurred? She has lulled these three children — her attendants — into quiet. A moment ago they were dancing and singing to your spell. Now under hers they sleep. I assure you, madam, that the spell you have just heard has placed a crowd of people vaster than any you can imagine under enchantment. For hours together they sit silent as your chicken here. Hearts of stone are moved to pity, and to similar spells a thousand men will march, if need be into the jaws of death."

Madam Melanie nodded her head. Her great blue eyes fixed themselves admiringly on Pansy. "A very strong spell," she said. "A spell that can send a thousand men to march to their deaths!" She took from her pocket a small pipe, lit it from a coal which she took from the fire with unflinching fingers and began to smoke contentedly, like one who has just made a good bargain and relishes the sensation.

# CHAPTER 14

*In which Pansy and Jenny without the assistance of witchcraft contrive a plan to outwit their captors.*

EDRO ALVAREZ and his men, having rested for a few days in the swamp, betook themselves on another expedition and Pansy and her friends saw no more of them. Though they could not be said to have given much pleasure with their presence, Pansy felt, and Captain Forsyth agreed with her, that their departure widened the gulf between themselves and the outside world. They were lost — they were, as the captain phrased it, living corpses, buried alive — and the world went on without them. Pedro assured the captain solemnly that the letters to the uncle in London would shortly start to wend their way across the Atlantic and that the captain was to enjoy his leisure until an answer could reasonably be expected. Then, taking Jack with him in order, he said, to train him up for a cabin boy, Pedro disappeared. There was a short, ugly scene when Jenny learned that Jack was to go. She clung fiercely to the boy until he himself rounded on her. He wished to go to sea. The pirates had been kind to him and when he was cold and tired they would give him rum and tobacco. He would become a rich man and come back and buy her, he said. He and Bill would both become pirate captains and own their ships and prey upon the fleets of the world. Bill cried that he might go too, but the captain said he was too small. He showed his kindest side at this time, giving Bill every assurance that his turn would come and he would be the fiercest pirate who ever sailed the seas. Then he bade Jenny stop her bawling and rode off in the wagon, with Mistress Melanie at the reins, leaving his prisoners in their compound and Jenny with her head in her apron.

Madam Melanie did not return for two days, and during that time Pansy and the Captain were free to explore their surroundings and learn to their dismay just how completely imprisoned they were. To leave the swamp without knowing the way out was so difficult as to be almost impossible and probably very dangerous. The cabin in which they lived stood on a slight rise of dry ground and was entirely surrounded by water save for one causeway. When Captain Forsyth ventured into the water he sank almost at once to his knees in stinking mud and only pulled himself out by grasping a root on the bank, so hauling himself to land again. Then the captain crossed the causeway on foot and walked for two hours through the thicket until he reached the point at which the party had left the barge. The pirates had taken the barge and the water was wide and deep. He told Pansy that the mists lay so thick that he could not see the other shore, and the alligators guarded the waters like sentries.

"We would not be more securely imprisoned if we had a troop of horse and a hundred men with muskets to keep us here," said Captain Forsyth. "We cannot make an escape fortuitously. We must plan it."

The hot, moist days were gloomy enough to have made stouter hearts than Pansy's faint, but the nights were terrifying. Strange whisperings filled the air and sharp, guttural cries from creatures which Pansy could scarcely imagine jarred the thick darkness, making her heart pound and causing her to draw her skirts around her for fear of some creeping thing, some snake lurking nearby or bat just overhead, watching her with wicked little eyes.

There were ceremonies among the people of the compound: small fires burned and figures danced about them, singing and stamping, and under it all there was the ceaseless beating of a drum.

"The living dead are playing," said Madam Melanie with her strange blue gaze fixed upon the mist as though she could see straight through it. Sometimes she joined the living dead but more often she crouched in the cabin, smoking and smiling at her own thoughts.

She told Pansy that she was the wife of Pedro and that one day they would rule all the world of the swamp together, and the great city at the mouth of the river.

"Someday he will sack it," said Madam Melanie. "There is much gold in New Orleans: Spanish gold. There are guns and kegs of rum in the governor's palace. I have seen the palace and one day I shall live there, when my spells have worked their way and Pedro has captured the town."

"The problem that confronts us, my dear Miss Scrooby," said Captain Forsyth, "is how to elude Mistress Melanie, who never appears to sleep, capture the barge, and make our way to New Orleans. From there our course is clear. We need only cast ourselves upon the mercy of the Governor, deliver the pirates and that Hell-hag to justice, which, you may be sure, will be swift, and take ship to England. The end is simplicity itself but the means defeat the imagination. And yet, you and I are intelligent and educated people and I see no reason why we should not outwit a handful of felons and a madwoman in the end. Is there not some ruse by which we can lull the suspicions of Mistress Melanie?"

"The driver who bought me from my dear Squire Scrooby was in mortal fear of me because he fancied me a witch," said Pansy. "I would that I could make Madam Melanie fear me too. She thinks me a witch but she thinks herself even more powerful. If I could *only* make it thunder or make the moon go down or animals to talk she might be too afraid to keep us here. As it is I cannot set foot outside this cabin but she is at my side, or one of those others — the living dead — they watch us all the time. But surely if we could steal the barge — they could not cross the water after us once we were away, and the rest would not be difficult."

It was as Pansy said. In spite of the loneliness of the swamp one was never alone. One crouched at the brink of the swamp water and knew that one of the swamp people was watching. Bats watched, owls watched, snakes watched and alligators watched. Madam Melanie, above all, watched with her blue eyes and laughed to herself and chanted snatches of songs and smoked her pipe.

Captain Forsyth fell prey to idleness. He had nothing with him save a change of clothing and he declared that he envied Pansy her sampler. She at least could stitch at it — and indeed did so until she finished it, while describing to Captain Forsyth how she had taught herself to read, using it as both slate and primer. She sang to Captain Forsyth to beguile his imprisonment and he rewarded her with prophecies of future triumphs when they should be released from captivity. Jenny, regarded by nobody, crept about the compound, gathered roots and berries when Madam Melanie ordered her to, and moped in a half-witted way, clucking at the chickens, which led to her being more and more ignored. Bill moped after her.

Thus it fell out that while Madam Melanie kept a vigilant watch over her little witch, as she was pleased to call Pansy, and never let her eyes stray from the captain, she allowed Jenny and Bill to melt into the landscape. They joined the living dead.

Pansy's singing fascinated the swamp queen. She would crouch staring from her place by the fire, listening as Pansy warbled and trilled. The captain, who had a light, tuneful voice, occasionally joined her, making a pleasant harmony. Madam Melanie laughed heartily to hear them sing together, and often wondered aloud at their spell-making, at the same time as she expressed doubts that it was very strong.

"You wish to get away from here but your spells do not remove you," she said scornfully.

"We are merciful people," retorted Captain Forsyth, "and do not wish to work too powerful a spell lest it injure you."

Madam Melanie laughed. Pansy set up another song, her old favorite, "To Anacreon in Heaven," and Jenny, who had been drifting about the compound all day in her soundless manner, came in and took up the place which she usually occupied in a far corner of the room. Pansy noticed that Jenny shivered and seemed unusually bedraggled. In fact when Pansy concluded her aria she saw on looking closer that Jenny was soaked to the skin and seemed chilled and rather frightened. It was late in the evening, and Madam Melanie arose and drew the wooden bar across the cabin door and composed herself for the night on the pile of corn husks near the fire which she used as a bed. It was the best bed in the cabin. The captives satisfied themselves with the floor, Pansy and the captain using their cloaks to keep out the damp.

In the darkness Pansy felt cold fingers sweep across her cheek and started up.

"Pansy!" Jenny's whisper was so low that Pansy could barely hear it. "The barge. I know where the barge is."

"Yes," whispered Pansy, "but what of it?"

"I know a way to bring it here. But I cannot do it alone. Two of us can bring it to the island. Will you come with me? I daren't call the captain. *She* would wake."

Silent as a kitten Pansy arose. Luckily she had removed her slippers when she lay down to sleep and she went barefoot now, lifting her petticoats high as she and Jenny slipped out the cabin door. The moon was riding high and after the darkness of the cabin the moonlit swamp seemed almost as bright as by daylight. Together the two children stole across the causeway and down the tree-lined avenue, keeping close to the edge of the path. Jenny went through the thicket at a dogtrot and Pansy kept pace with her, remembering the swift trot of the impala in her African days under that same tropical moon.

Jenny ran swiftly and more swiftly, her thin legs moving rapidly under her short ragged petticoats. Pansy had more trouble as her wet ruffles dragged at her ankles, and she was forced to stop finally and gird up her skirts with her kerchief ties. The swamp rang with night sounds, with the whirring of insects and the owl's cry and the call of night-hawks. And everywhere Pansy was aware — or thought she was aware — of the presence of the living dead. They were staring at her with dull eyes from the swamp forest and were bound to betray her. The very thought of them filled her with terror — and kept her on her feet and running.

An hour of this swift foot travel brought the girls to the waterway and there, moored to the little dock, was the barge where Madam Melanie had left it. Pansy and Jenny ran down the dock and leaped to the deck. Jenny, who had evidently practiced this move, untied the barge from its moorings, caught at the pole, and maneuvered the awkward craft toward an inlet which gaped like a small gullet and led back into the swamp.

The barge slid smoothly into the stream and glided down the water leaving scarcely a ripple in its wake. Pansy stood forward, parting the branches which impeded its progress, while Jenny poled in the stern. If the run to the river had been frightening, Pansy thought, the journey through the swamp was ten times worse and this time she had not the comfort of running. Several times the stream became so narrow that she thought the barge would be wedged between the two banks and would be stuck fast. She and Jenny leaned on the pole until their shoulders seemed about to burst from their sockets — and then the barge shot so swiftly into the wider part of the stream that both girls nearly lost their footing. And to fall into the water here was to meet an unimaginable fate. For they poled their way through whole communities of alligators whose eyes with their upward-closing lids seemed to carry worlds of cruel stupidity. The trailing moss from the trees waved about the girls' heads, touching their cheeks, twitching at their clothing, and caressing the backs of their necks like the fingers of a ghost.

Everything seemed to be something that it wasn't. Roots looked like snakes and snakes like roots. A rock, startled, swam hideously away into the mud and a huge turtle proved to be nothing but a rock. The dawn came up and with it the mist — and with the dawn Pansy and Jenny poled to the edge of the island where the cabin stood.

"Fetch Bill: I shall fetch the captain and we will go," said Pansy. "It is still scarcely daylight. It must be now or we shall never escape from the swamp."

She jumped from the barge and Jenny sped after her and up the rickety steps of the cabin. All was dark within. Pansy groped her way to where the captain lay and set her hand across his lips. She felt him stir in the darkness and laid her lips to his ear telling him to come forthwith, that a boat lay at the sill. He started up and together they reached the cabin door where Jenny stood, with Bill riding on her back and fortunately half asleep.

Then Pansy turned and in the half light she saw the voodoo queen rise to her feet and look about her. "Run!" screamed Pansy. Captain Forsyth, after one backward look, wasted no time. He ran, but not to the barge. Instead he flung himself against the cabin door and slammed it to, knocking Pansy over so that she rolled down the bank where Jenny, standing with the pole, caught her. The captain then made the barge in two leaps but the voodoo queen came down the bank screaming, her kerchief torn from her head in her flight and her bushy red-gold hair

standing out around her face like a fire. Jenny poled furiously but she could not pull the barge into the middle of the stream quickly enough to stop Madam Melanie from leaping aboard. Suddenly the barge stood midstream with the voodoo queen, the captain, Pansy, Jenny and Bill drifting into the current. The woman screamed for her people.

They came to the edge of the stream, drifting like swamp moss, like mist, from their quarters in the underbrush. They stood dark and listless against the swamp growth. They could not help their mistress. They could not reach the barge and Jenny poled into the narrow stream which led back to the wider water while the voodoo queen chanted and waved in vain. From the mud the alligators stared unmoving and indifferent.

"Heaven preserve us!" gasped the captain, "and keep these creatures at our side! They will protect us from every interference. Madam, I must warn you that the faintest disposition on your part to incommode us on our little journey will lead to your being flung without ceremony to yonder creatures — who will not, I fancy, have the least hesitation in devouring you piecemeal. You were good enough to suggest that *we* might garnish their repast. I fancy you yourself might make better eating than my young friends here, who in point of size are scarcely worth the trouble of dressing for the table."

Madam Melanie glared down at the swamp waters and then at the captain.

"I shall be revenged," she said angrily. "Pedro Alvarez will avenge me."

"I think it most unlikely," said the captain. "We shall pursue our way at once to New Orleans where you, as a woman of sense will, I feel certain, find it much more convenient to maintain good humor and discretion if you do not wish to adorn a gallows. As for Pedro, his doom is sealed. You are as good as a handsome widow already and I advise you to make the best of it. There are worse states under the sun and with any luck Pedro will have left you something in the way of money or goods. You need only guide us to New Orleans and I think I may promise you that I shall see that things go not so hard with you as you deserve. Any failure to comply with this request of course cancels the bargain. Jenny, give me the pole. We shall see the governor's palace by midday, I trust."

# CHAPTER 15

*In which Sophia Scrooby visits the Old World and through the kind offices of Captain Forsyth is received into the best society.*

TO ENTER the city of New Orleans was, for Pansy, like reliving a remote part of her past life. Here was a town of the New World which resembled Moçambique, with its palm trees and steaming heats and bright, blue waters. Its white buildings were blinding in the sun and its populace chattered three languages, French, English and Spanish, as though they were trying to create one language out of the three.

In New Haven people moved swiftly, intent on their business, but here they sauntered through the hot streets or stopped to refresh themselves in the dark taverns as though they had nothing better to do than breathe the scent of magnolias, gossip, drink wine and eat prawns all the livelong day.

Upon reaching the city Captain Forsyth at once put up at a tavern. Pansy could not but admire the arrangements he made for himself. His first transaction was to sell the barge.

"Money, my dear Sophia," he said, "may be the root of all evil, but it is also an extraordinarily convenient thing to possess. I could, I suppose, sell you — or perhaps Mistress Melanie — but since I am unalterably opposed to trafficking in human flesh it seems both more pleasant and more in accordance with my principles to deal in stolen goods. The barge should fetch us the price of a gentleman's lodging for a few days and then we shall see what we shall see. You must have a new gown and a fashionable cap."

"What do you intend to do with Madam Melanie?" asked Pansy, very curious.

"Send her straight to the devil. She shall go free. The means of hanging herself will no doubt present themselves in due course. Humane considerations prevent me from handing her over to the authorities here, who might take it upon themselves to burn her as a witch. No, let her go, I say. Her paramour is on the high seas where the authorities will inevitably find him, sooner or later. It will be enough for us to restore our fallen fortunes. I propose to return to England where I shall write my memoirs. What do you propose?"

"I must find my way to Canada and rescue my family."

"You are everything that is amiable, my dear young lady. However, allow me to point out to you a few insuperable obstacles to your mission in its present form. I dislike discussing unpleasant matters but there is one fact which I feel I should mention. You are at present, under the laws of your country, the property of a slaver — a chattel, no more than a heifer to be sold at market. Canada is a vast and chilly waste, populated largely by Indians, who are, as I understand, little better than heathen — downright Dissenters, ma'am. The rest of the population is French. Need I say more? Now attend to me. I shall take you to England. I shall address myself to the pleasing task of educating you. You have made excellent progress so far. You will of course study music. You will see London and all the refinements of civilization, inseparable from London life. I shall turn you into the finest little lady in six counties. You will sing your way into the hearts of all. Think, Sophia! You will be in a much better state to rescue the Scrooby family if you have position and fortune, which my efforts and your attainments will almost certainly acquire for you."

"And Jenny and Bill, sir? I could not abandon them in this strange town. It would be unfaithful and unfeeling."

"Jenny is a capable and useful girl. She will travel with you as your attendant. You will require one in any case. Bill is a bit young for service but I have an aunt in Greenwich who would fancy a page. Yes, decidedly, Bill shall go to my aunt. He will look well in powder. She will spoil him but he will enjoy that."

"And shall we then be your slaves, sir?" asked Pansy, hesitantly.

"Nay, Sophia, the law will not allow it. You may be worse — for I shall make you a ward in Chancery. This is one of the refinements of civilization of which I spoke. It is a fate which befalls many young ladies of quality so you will be no worse than they. Nay, do not look so chapfallen. You have crossed the broad Atlantic in a slave ship, you have served in the house of Pharaoh, if I may be permitted the comparison. Now you are in sight of the promised land — to continue the metaphor. That it turns out to be ruled from the woolsack is scarcely my fault. Favor me with one of your smiles, my dear young lady. As my ward you will come to the distinguished attention of the Lord Chancellor and will meet the best people in the best circumstances. I shall take you to Vauxhall. You will see fireworks, fêtes, hear music, observe lords and ladies at their innocent amusements, and if you are truly virtuous I shall present you to a duchess. She is a stupid old thing but yet she is a duchess. And when you are twenty-one years old you will be your own mistress and may travel where you please without let or hindrance. You were good enough to rescue me in adversity. I shall not let you return to the condition of a slave."

"And when I am rich and free and famous I may find the Scroobys again?"

"I honor your faithful heart and I think it very likely."

"I should be a monster of ingratitude," said Pansy slowly — she was usually forced to conduct her conversations with the captain slowly in order to match words with him, since he had such a gigantic supply — "if I did not comply with the dictates of — of your noble heart. And if you will rescue Jenny and Bill too —" she looked up at the captain. As usual he was half laughing. He was always half laughing, but he had indeed a noble heart.

And so it turned out that after some weeks in New Orleans during which time the captain completed arrangements for the voyage, Pansy with Jenny and Bill set sail for England in the care of Captain Forsyth. His adventures with the pirates had aroused a great deal of sympathy in the bosom of the Spanish governor of New Orleans and every assistance was given the Englishman to get his passage home.

The captain said that his months in the swamps had spoiled his appetite for adventure. He wanted no further wandering but would return to England to pursue a profession.

"And what profession will you pursue?" inquired Pansy.

"The law and the church have both appealed to me," said the captain, "but I fear this is because I am addicted to the use of words. Harrying poor devils to death in the courts might come to bore me. The church might lead to marriage and life in the country, for which no opportunities for rhetoric would suffice to console me. Therefore I cannot enter the law or the church. I have had my taste of military life, I have small means and so I think I shall live by my wits."

"That is not a profession, sir," said Pansy cautiously.

"No? Well, I shall become a poet, a builder of romantic ruins, in short, Miss Scrooby, a student of life itself. What do you think of that for a profession?"

"It sounds an interesting one, sir," said Pansy. She thought it would suit her, too, but she feared it might not bring in enough money to return to Canada and for all her gratitude to the captain and her affection for Jenny and Bill her thoughts remained fixed upon a very northern star. As the ship on which she traveled sailed eastward she often came up on deck and looked upward to where the North Star hung in the sky. Captain Forsyth had pointed out the constellations to her and she enjoyed picking out stars and planets and fancying that somewhere Prudence was doing the same thing and longing for her as she longed for her family. She wondered especially how Mr. Scrooby fared and if Prudence had learned to read and if she was patient enough to read to her father. She mentioned in her prayers that this would be a good thing for Prudence to do and did not fail to remind the Lord mornings and evenings to nudge Prudence to perform her duty in this regard.

The ship had a calm and uneventful voyage. Captain Forsyth was apprehensive about pirates after his disagreeable experience but none appeared. Save for one heavy storm as they approached the shores of England the weather was good. The storm was a serious one and caused the ship's officers to look grave but Pansy and the other two children thoroughly enjoyed it. The chests slid down the cabin floors and Bill rode them, whooping triumphantly as he slid across the boards. But the weather cleared at last and the ship sailed her way majestically one bright morning into Bristol Harbor where Pansy saw the coast of England, green and smiling under the sun.

"A most unusual day," remarked Captain Forsyth. "I can only say, Sophia, that your arrival occurs most auspiciously. It nearly always rains here. Good weather is all but unheard of on first arriving in England."

"It is a very pretty day," said Pansy. She and Jenny were pressed against the rail, straining their eyes for every possible view of England. The disembarkation was festive in the sunshine and Pansy and her companions found themselves the center of a most enjoyable scene. As Pansy was handed down the ship's ladder by Captain Forsyth and set foot on British soil she heard a murmur of admiration from the bystanders. They seemed to be staring respectfully and Pansy heard a woman turn to a neighbor and murmur something about a foreign princess.

"You see, Miss Scrooby," said the captain, "they take you for an African princess arriving with your highness's retinue. Oblige them with a bow. Kiss your hand to them. They expect it."

Flushing with shyness and pleasure, Pansy bowed and kissed her hand. Jenny bobbed a curtsy and Bill, not to be outdone, whipped off the striped stocking cap which one of the sailors had given him and made a deep bow.

The crowd was delighted. "Oh what a little jackanapes! See the pretty fellow. Oh, Mammy, has he come to live with us?"

But there was no time to make the acquaintance of all of these people. The captain took his charges to an inn called the White Lion where they caused another stir. Jenny and Pansy managed to keep their composure but Bill, who had never had so much attention before, quite lost his head. He gave a show while waiting for the London coach and when it arrived at the inn door he danced a hornpipe down the path to meet it. He strutted and cheered and hitched up his trousers sailor fashion, until Jenny, exasperated with all these airs, fetched him a clout across the ear to remind him whose little brother he was. The coach was announced, and somewhat sobered and with his ears ringing Bill took his place on the box beside a stout coachman. Pansy, Jenny and the captain settled themselves inside the carriage which was to take them to London.

All that Pansy had heard and read of England seemed to unfold itself beyond the windows of the carriage. Flowers sprang, larks trilled and spires rose above feathery trees. Cottages with thatched roofs nestled among green leaves and from time to time the turrets and chimneys of some great house appeared at a distance. They paused several times to change horses and well before sundown they reached Bath, where the captain insisted on their stopping for the night. The captain explained that this green and pleasant land was infested with highwaymen and footpads.

"You would not care to lose all your jewels at the hands of some celebrated MacHeath, madam," he said. "You have preserved that coral necklace from pirates and West Indian witches. It would be a thousand pities to lose it to a hardy British malefactor before your first day here is out."

"That would be quite shocking," said Pansy, but in spite of the pious sentiment she could not help longing a little to see a highwayman. She had often read that they were very gallant, bold fellows who were enormously polite while taking ladies' watches. However, one of the few things that Pansy did not see on her way to London was a highwayman.

The second and third days of the journey offered a fine variety of scenery and towards the end of the day a change from pastures and hills and streams. The sky became hazy and Pansy's nose began to wrinkle and twitch at the strange smell which arose.

"You smell London, I see," said the captain. "We are approaching the city. Jenny, be so good as to pull down the window shades."

"Are we not to see London?" asked Pansy.

"Oh you shall see London, right enough. But we will soon be coming by Temple Bar. There is yet one traitor's head — the last but one fell in 1772. Times change and one day we may do without these adornments."

"But whose heads are they?" asked Pansy. "And how long have they been there?"

"They are the rebels of forty-five. The heads remain

until they fall. How curious you are! You surely don't care to see such a sight?"

"Oh, no," said Pansy. "I should hate it. It seems a barbarous thing to do. Don't they smell?"

"London smells," said Captain Forsyth. "It is the way of cities. We shall not detain ourselves here. I am taking you to Greenwich to my aunt's. I trust she will be as delighted to see us as I shall be to accept the luxury of her premises for a short period of time. We are bound to entertain her. She lives an extremely tedious existence between church-going and gambling and we should offer her a great deal of diversion by our mere presence."

"Your aunt gambles, sir?" asked Pansy.

"What else should she do for amusement? She is too old and too stout to venture often to the theater and besides has an unholy dread of being set upon by felons. She is neither educated nor intelligent but she is extremely kind and much inclined to company. As an aunt she has proved invaluable to me on any number of occasions and I am hoping for a great deal of comfort in her household at this time when I arrive at her door travel-sore and weary after countless adventures. She has a fine house in Greenwich with a view of the river. The air is salubrious, the garden a pleasant place to dally, and my aunt keeps a good cook. You may pull up the blind now, Sophia. We have passed Temple Bar. Look behind you and you will see Paul's dome."

Pansy peered out the window and saw the great pearl of London pale and shimmering among the chimneys and the needle spires of other churches. The city was vaster than anything she had experienced save possibly Africa, which

194

had dwindled in her imagination. She gave a gulp at the sheer hugeness of London. Now they had left the city and were among trees and gardens again. The Thames shone intermittently in its course. The coach bowled up to a house — a red brick house, neither large nor small but just the right size — and came to a stop.

"Now for my aunt," said Captain Forsyth. "Wait in the coach, children, while I announce our arrival."

The captain disappeared up the steps and after about twenty minutes he reappeared. He was wreathed in smiles. Behind him in the doorway stood an elderly lady. She was the most fanciful lady Pansy had ever seen. She wore a rich lavender frock with an enormous hoop and a high head-dress of powdered hair surmounted with feathers. She was decked in lace and ribbons and brooches, she wore black lace mitts, and she fluttered a tortoiseshell fan. She was twittering like a sparrow with excitement and curiosity.

"Bring them in, John. Are they not odd! Are they not dark! Do they speak English? Oh, what strange little people! Oh, John!"

Pansy stepped from the carriage, twitched up her skirts above her ankles and tripped up the steps. On the threshold she made an elegant curtsy.

"And so you are the little *belle sauvage*," said the lady, smiling graciously.

"No, madam," said Pansy, smiling with equal graciousness. "A little American."

# CHAPTER 16

*In which Pansy Scrooby learns about London life. She is introduced to the pleasures of the card table and the town, and encounters a new friend.*

ISS PAMELA FORSYTH was a lady of sixty-odd who had once been a beauty. She had been by her own account so remarkable a beauty that it was quite a wonder, Pansy thought, that nobody had won her for a wife, but as she explained when Pansy asked her, she was also very cold and cruel and no suitor had ever touched her heart.

"And therefore, my dear Sophia," said the old lady, "both heart and fortune remained intact. My admirers might content themselves as best they would with the affections of others. For my part, I am very well satisfied."

Miss Forsyth had been in her youth a maid of honor to the Princess of Wales and had mightily enjoyed the post. She had a fund of tales of court life, mostly about what people wore and how much money they lost at cards. Whole fortunes, farms, estates, inheritances went careening across the gaming tables and Pansy's eyes grew large and round to hear it. England was a truly startling country by comparison with which both Africa and America seemed quite tame.

Pansy's eyes would widen and from time to time she expressed severe disapproval of the goings-on in London.

She had been far too piously brought up by the Scroobys not to feel that Miss Forsyth was terribly frivolous and vain, and that so many people, dancing and gambling their lives away, might have to answer for these things in a future state. Miss Forsyth went off into peals of laughter at Pansy's sermons. She called her a comical little colonial and told her naughty story after naughty story while Pansy, dressed in white ruffles and scarlet ribbons, shook her head and clicked her tongue.

But for all her gaiety and frivolity Miss Forsyth was lonely. Although her nephew, the captain, was dutiful he was also young and could not be with her a great deal, and at sixty she was no longer plagued with suitors. So the arrival of Pansy, first as a visitor and then as a permanent companion which she shortly became, was in the nature of a gift from Heaven. By the time Pansy had been with Miss Forsyth six weeks the lady often remarked that she did not know how she had ever managed without her.

Miss Forsyth was good-natured enough to make life pleasant for those who lived with her provided that they kept her entertained, and Jenny and Bill both learned this very soon also. She dressed Bill up in a white silk suit with a sea-green turban and started to train him for a page. Bill combed her lapdog, a fluffy, yapping little spaniel called Fido; he handed tea about when ladies called and cut capers with the little boys who hung about Miss Forsyth's kitchen. Jenny attended principally on Pansy but spent many hours embroidering Miss Forsyth's petticoats and flounces, a skill which Pansy had taught her. The old lady adored clothes, and all the female members of her household, when they weren't quarreling among themselves, passed the greater portion of their time in washing, ironing and getting up caps, frocks and lace ruffles.

Miss Forsyth was enchanted with Pansy's singing and after dinner, which took place about four o'clock in the afternoon, usually enjoyed a concert. In fact the presence of Pansy much enlarged Miss Forsyth's social life because her friends came to drink tea with her and to gape at the *belle sauvage* as they called Pansy, and to congratulate Miss Forsyth on her nephew's thoughtfulness in providing his aunt with so unusual a companion. They all affected great sensibility, as Miss Forsyth said, and wept comfortably at all Pansy's sad songs but she could not help noticing how rapidly they recovered from their tears when supper was served and the tables set out for cards.

But Miss Forsyth could not give musical evenings every night in the week and she was sometimes forced to dine alone with Pansy, and after she had heard all that Pansy had to tell her of her history, of her life in the African village and her journey to the colonies, by which Miss Forsyth meant every part of the world except London, and after the old lady had called for her salts over the pirates and had her stays loosened at the account of Madam Melanie, Pansy had to think up new amusements. Just as she began to wrinkle her brow over what to tell Miss Forsyth next and had even considered making up a few stories, Miss Forsyth looked at her sharply through her lorgnon and cried:

"Bless my soul, Sophia, but you don't know how to play cards!" as though she had observed this dreadful lack in Pansy for the first time.

"No, madam," replied Pansy. "Squire Scrooby did not care for cards."

"Tut-tut," said the old lady fussily. "I can't think how he passed the time."

"He was blind, as I have told you," said Pansy. "I read and sang to him."

"You observed that he was often melancholy," said Miss Forsyth. "It came of too much reading, I haven't a doubt, and though I dote on music, as you know, Sophia, one wants a little merriment. I shall teach you to play. Thus we may while away the evenings. Ring for the candles and the cards, Sophia. We shall take a hand together."

And thus it was that Pansy learned card playing. There was as it turned out very little that Miss Forsyth did not know about it. She taught Pansy loo, whist, quadrille, *vingt-et-un* and faro.

Pansy learned these games quite quickly and evening after evening she sat opposite the old lady, shuffling and dealing and learning the ways of the gaming table. Miss Forsyth was in ecstasies. Pansy was so quick that she soon became a very worthy opponent. After a while Miss Forsyth, wearying of a game in which there was no risk, began playing for small stakes. She provided Pansy with a small allowance in order to win it from her in the evenings. Pansy found at first that this was amusing but she soon wearied of seeing her few shillings a week go back into Miss Forsyth's purse. She bent her mind to the game and took to winning. She was a good card player and was of a much sharper wit than Miss Forsyth. Her shillings began to turn into pounds. Captain Forsyth would come and stand over the table, studying the hands and occasionally giving advice, quite fairly. He did not favor one lady over another but he offered instruction to both from which Pansy especially profited. The play grew quite lively and as Pansy's little dark hands raked in the takings Captain Forsyth would fling himself onto one of his aunt's sofas and laugh until the glass drops on the chandelier rang. Miss Forsyth took to giving Pansy small notes-in-hand acknowledging her debts, which Pansy kept carefully in a small silver box which the captain brought her one day, just so, he said, she might keep a strict account of the moneys owing her. Pansy kept a conscientious account. She had one end in view for this money. It would buy her freedom in America and enable her to restore the Scroobys to their home and herself to them. It justified gambling and she no longer felt guilty about playing cards for money.

For in spite of the easy, luxurious life Pansy was not happy in Miss Forsyth's agreeable home. Although she was far too deep in the old lady's favor and the captain's for the servants to abuse her, she suffered from their jealousy. The haughty lady's maid, Miss Hester, gave her cold looks and spoke of her as "that blackamoor." She did not dare do it to Pansy's face but Pansy often overheard her whispering with the chambermaids about their mistress's folly. Pansy knew that had they dared they would have turned her and Jenny out of the house without a rag to their backs nor a penny to hand, and sometimes she fell a prey to fearful anxiety lest some disaster befall either Miss Forsyth or the captain. To be turned out of doors so near London was a nightmare which haunted her nights and darkened her days. Vice and wickedness were everywhere in the city. She had seen men flogged through the streets, and she had seen gibbets on Tyburn with malefactors swinging in their chains. Women and children begged in the streets and hideous cripples with odious deformities pulled at her skirts when she descended from the sedan chair in which she occasionally accompanied Miss Forsyth on her visits. And Miss Forsyth's idle ways were tedious. Pansy longed for lessons, for Master Anthony's sums if nothing better would offer. Her best solace was her music. She had Miss Forsyths' pianoforte at her disposal and she employed nearly all of her leisure at practice. Miss Forsyth, who played and sang no more than a raven, nevertheless had a fine library of music and Pansy set herself to learning many new songs as well as refurbishing her old ones.

"I must get you a music master," said Miss Forsyth. "Such talent must not be neglected. Are you ready for our game, Sophia?" Pansy became more and more certain that, as before, she must find a music master for herself. In the meantime Pansy continued to sing as a bird sings, because she could find no other way to pour out her heart.

She was not always sad. The captain brought considerable pleasure into her life and unlike his aunt who merely thought she liked music he genuinely admired Pansy's singing.

"You may yet make my fortune, Sophia," he observed. "I have been speaking of you about town and some of Aunt's cronies are pleased to be pleased with your singing. You are becoming quite the thing this season. Soon we shall put it about that unless you have heard the little savage sing you can scarcely lay claim to any *ton* whatever. How should you like to sing at Drury Lane?"

"At Drury Lane, sir?"

"Yes, at Drury Lane. I know a capital fellow there who is always looking for something new to lay before the audience. You should do well at Drury Lane. You might do an interlude between two acts of *The Rivals*. I shall speak to my friend Sheridan of you, and to Doctor Burney."

He left Pansy to ponder the prospect of Drury Lane. How much, she wondered, did one earn by singing at Drury Lane. Perhaps one might sing for the King and then one would earn a great deal. It was a better way of earning a living than gambling with Miss Forsyth, for although Pansy was the better player and infinitely more cautious, she had to acknowledge that occasionally Miss Forsyth had an unexpected run of good cards. One could not hold aces, kings, queens and knaves all the time. Pansy considered triumphs at Drury Lane and waited for the captain to appear and say that he had made an appointment with the manager.

The captain however was invited to shoot grouse in Scotland and went off to visit a baronet in the highlands and did not pay his usual respects at Greenwich. Several weeks passed and Pansy grew impatient. The year was drawing to a close and she was not making any progress even to Drury Lane, much less Canada.

It was November and the sun never shone. Pansy began to feel as she had once felt in Africa: "Nothing ever happens here." She felt as though she had been cooped up in Miss Forsyth's house for twenty years.

Then one day at the beginning of Advent — Miss Forsyth was rather particular in her observation of feasts and fasts: she said it gave variety to her days — the old lady announced her intention of passing a few days at the house of a friend in London.

"We are dull without John Forsyth, are we not?" said Miss Forsyth. "I have a fancy to attend Divine Service at St. Paul's. We shall hear a fine, eloquent sermon and observe the winter fashions." Pansy thought how Prudence would have liked the winter fashions and smiled. Miss Forsyth made as much fuss over the journey from Greenwich to London as she would have created over an expedition to the North Pole. Two coaches were required to transport her and her belongings and Miss Hester, Pansy, Jenny, Bill and Fido. The journey was accomplished, however, by daylight and without incident; the coaches arrived in London in time for supper. The party had intended to reach its destination by midday but owing to the difficulties of carrying Miss Forsyth's clothes it was well past noon by the time the party got under way and near sundown by the time Miss Forsyth and her retinue were settled in with Lady Mary Barton, an old schoolfellow of Miss Forsyth's.

But once at Lady Mary's elegant house in London life went on much as usual although since Lady Mary lived in town rather than in countrified Greenwich she had a much greater store of gossip than Miss Forsyth was able to lay claim to. The old ladies chatted of the new house at Twickenham built by a gentleman named Walpole, exactly like an ancient castle, with battlements and turrets complete. Pansy quite longed to see the place. They talked of the court — the King was behaving very oddly and was no doubt a great trial to dear Queen Charlotte. They talked of the fashions from France and new parlor plaything called the *camera obscura* which did tricks with light. They complained of the high wages and impertinence of servants and the wicked ways of young people. And they gambled with other old ladies and gentlemen who came to call. These fussed and clucked over Pansy as though she were some newfangled doll or monkey and she was always glad to sing for them in order to gain a little peace for herself. Occasionally she found amusement in playing at riddles with this company — they doted on riddles — but she was afraid of taking a hand at cards here. Some of these people played a remarkably shrewd game and Pansy did not intend to lose money among these acquaintances.

"The round of pleasure which we are witnessing," said Pansy to Jenny, "distracts the mind and makes me, for one, weary and cross. Amusements can become quite tedious. Do you not agree?"

Jenny nodded her head in its white ruffled cap. She did not however agree. She was enjoying herself in London. She was beginning to make friends in Lady Mary's household and she hoped the visit would last.

"I have a mind for a walk," continued Pansy.

"Where will you walk?" asked Jenny. "We might become lost. London is very large."

"Only a little way. Surely if we step out of doors and explore a few streets we cannot lose ourselves. Let us fetch our cloaks."

Jenny thought it a bold venture but agreed that a short expedition could do no harm. The girls fetched their

hoods and then, seeing that the two old ladies were occupied in their unceasing dialogue in the morning room,
Pansy and Jenny sallied into the London streets.

It was a mild afternoon and the sun was faintly visible in
a white sky. Pansy and Jenny walked down the street,
crossed it and came to another street. The neighborhood
was a pleasant one. A few passers-by smiled down at the
two little foreigners who were quite clearly delighted with
their adventure. They bought lavender from a woman
who was crying her wares and stopped to admire a man
with a performing dog. The man and the dog moved
slowly from street to street and the dog was so full of pretty
tricks that Pansy and Jenny followed them and threw
farthings which the dog cleverly caught in his mouth.

"Pansy," said Jenny suddenly, "where are we?" Pansy
looked around her. Jenny was right. The neighborhood
had altered. They had wandered out of the pretty streets
and into another London. Everything was different. The
neat housefronts with their white steps and fan-shaped
windows over the entrances were gone. Here the houses
were darker and taller and the people too were changed.
There were more of them and they were less friendly than
the inhabitants of the pretty streets which the girls had
left.

"We must turn back," said Pansy. "We are not far from
home. Let us turn into this street here." They turned into
it but it was not the street from which they had come. A
beggar teased them for alms and a thin dog scuttled past
them as though escaping from some dreadful fate. They
passed a tavern and an unkempt woman who was hanging

out some kind of flag called after them, laughing shrilly —
they did not hear what she said but quickened their steps.
They ran down this street and came all at once upon a
knot of boys and men idling at a street corner. Pansy and
Jenny could not pass.

"See here," called one of the men. "What have we with
us?" He spoke with so ugly an accent that the girls could
scarcely understand him and as they shrank back he swaggered up to them and looked down from under fierce
eyebrows.

"Very finely dressed!" exclaimed the man. "Something
new in these parts. And these are very rare birds, too.
From India I should think — or the China seas." He took
hold of Pansy's cloak. "That is a fine cloak, mistress. I'll
have it off of you, I thank you."

"No, no. Be off with you!" said Pansy. Looking up she
saw that she was surrounded by a collection of the most
villainous and dirty people she had ever seen in her life.
There were angry, half-clothed women and children, who
were certainly starving. They were mopping and mowing
about her and reaching out their hands for her cloak.

"Let us pass, good people!" cried Pansy. "Let us pass, or
we shall summon a constable."

The crowd took this statement as a most delightful
witticism. "A constable. The little blackamoor will call a
constable. Come, blackamoor. Where did you steal that
cloak — and the necklace. We'll have a constable here and
you in Newgate." They were all about her. They were
pulling at Jenny too and had already taken her cloak from
her. Pansy heard her scream as a ruffian seized her muff
and tossed it to a woman who was sitting in a nearby

doorway, drinking from a bottle and watching the struggle greedily.

"Help us!" screamed Jenny. "Somebody help us!"

"Now what is all this?" This was a different voice. Someone had come. A gentleman was standing over the mob with an upraised cane. "Off, be off with you, I say! Fie, for shame!"

He was a very large, stout man, well wrapped up against the weather. He had a commanding manner and a ringing

voice. The mob dropped their game. "No more, no more, I say!" cried the voice. "Now, young ladies, how came you here?"

"Oh, thank you, sir," cried Pansy. "Oh, sir, my friend and I were merely walking abroad for a moment and now we are lost." She looked up into the face of her benefactor and gave a start. Standing there in lace and ruffles, his tall cane in his hand, a brilliant smile on his broad face, was a gigantic African.

"Come, little lady," he said. "Come to my shop. It is but a step from this unpleasant alley. Come with me. Ignatius Sancho, at your service. And who may you be?"

# CHAPTER 17

*In which Sophia Scrooby is reunited with old friends.*

E SHALL PROCEED to my shop," said Mr. Sancho. "And there you may recount to me the story of your adventures. We shall also take measures to restore you to your friends. Kindly follow me and avoid the loose cobbles. My shop is in Charles Street."

Charles Street proved to be a walk of about twenty minutes but it was not accomplished without event. For one thing Mr. Sancho seemed to have a vast acquaintance — almost everyone in London, Pansy concluded. He stopped every few minutes and talked with friends whom he greeted enthusiastically; after a cordial exchange of compliments and embraces conversation ensued. Mr. Sancho appeared to be something of a politician and a patron of the arts as well as a churchwarden and prosperous tradesman. He was also, as he explained, interested in reform. Pansy was about to enquire what kind of reform he undertook when a carter appeared from around a corner, driving a donkey who staggered under a heavy load of firewood. The carter was swearing and whipping the donkey unmercifully. He had barely raised his whip however when Mr. Sancho was in the street, his tall gold-headed cane upraised.

"Fie upon you, my man! Fie, I say! It is one of God's creatures. How dare you abuse it so. Stop it, sirrah, or you will taste my cane."

The carter was too astonished for a moment to make a reply and before he had regained his wits Mr. Sancho was off on a lecture of which the gist was that the man would be impressed to fight the Americans if he ever again was caught abusing the donkey. The great golden voice of Mr. Sancho poured out a flood of words, threats, arguments. The carter tried to argue that the donkey was his. Mr. Sancho never heard him. The donkey stood, like the ass in the Bible before the angel, shaking his ears, and Mr. Sancho, after breaking the man's whip, tossed it aside and allowed the carter to pass with a final warning of the fate that lay in store for those who were cruel to their beasts of burden.

In this manner after several more delays, to give alms to beggars, to pet stray cats, to offer assistance to a blind man and to chat with several small boys, they finally reached Mr. Sancho's shop.

It was a grocery shop, but it more resembled the hold of a galleon sailing out of the Indies than any ordinary grocer's shop. Mr. Sancho carried spices from the Far East, saffron, cloves and cinnamon. There were wines from France and Spain gleaming from shelves in one corner of the shop. There were truffles and Strasbourg geese, fine pastries, cheeses, pineapples, game from Scotland, hothouse vegetables from the gardens of Kent and Surrey; there were candied citrons, Devonshire strawberries, Moor Park apricots and crocks of clotted cream. Pansy and Jenny had never seen such an array of delicacies. Mr.

Sancho sat them down on a little settle and then plied them with morsels of sweet and morsels of spice, oddments that scarcely tasted like food at all and yet were too delicious not to eat.

"So you hail from the colonies —" Mr. Sancho had somehow managed to absorb this information from the girls in the course of their walk together. "Let me assure you now that I have no sympathy with your cause, no sympathy whatsoever. I am averse to any form of enthusiasm. Further, you maintain the institution of slavery. But I should not rebuke you. You have no doubt experienced this evil in your own persons. In short, my dears, you are the victims, not the perpetrators. Are you not fortunate to have found yourselves here! Have a little more marzipan. It is very wholesome. It is possible that generations from now may see a better America, a great nation, rising like Rome from small beginnings — but I cannot countenance rebellion. Better to make peace and pay her taxes and free her slaves. But I run on too long and have not asked you where your friends are to be found. They are no doubt distracted at your loss, not knowing that you are safe and sound. You should not venture into the streets alone, dressed so fine. You are a walking temptation to thieves." Pansy tried to explain that they had lost themselves only a little way from Lady Mary Barton's town house.

"Lady Mary Barton," said Mr. Sancho. "Lady Mary Barton. She is not one of my regular customers, I believe. No matter. Mrs. Sancho will know. She keeps our accounts. We were speaking of America. I have never seen it, although I was briefly in South America. I was in fact baptized there. Like yourselves I was once a slave. Good fortune brought me here to London at the age of two so I have no recollection of it. Tell me, how do you like London? How do you entertain yourselves?"

"We like it very well," answered Pansy. "We live with a kind lady and serve her. But there is not much entertainment. We embroider and I play at cards with Miss Forsyth."

"Gambling, my dear child! Heaven forbid! At your age? You must not play at cards. I gambled myself in youth. A disgraceful episode. I lost shockingly at cards. Tell me, are you fond of the theater?"

"I think we should be," replied Pansy. "I am sure we should dote on it. But we have never seen a play. I myself love music. I sing and play but we have no opportunity to go to the theater."

"I shall take you to the theater at once," said Mr. Sancho. "I am attending Mrs. Siddons tonight in her performance of Lady Macbeth in one of the masterpieces of William Shakespeare. I trust you are fond of Shakespeare."

"Oh, extremely," said Pansy, and she and Jenny both nodded vigorously.

"I have acted myself," said Mr. Sancho. "Unfortunately I was not blessed with talent. Fortune finally found me in this grocery business which has flourished in a particularly blessed manner. I have the patronage of some of the finest houses in England. Lady Mary Barton. I shall take you back to Lady Mary myself. I shall send a messenger to say that you are safely in my hands. But if we go round by Lady Mary's we shall be late for Mrs. Siddon's entrance and that I could not endure. You shall see Mrs. Siddons and then we shall repair to your place of residence. Are you ready?"

There was no more resisting Mr. Sancho than if he had been a hurricane. Pansy and Jenny said that they were quite ready.

He thrust an orange into the hand of each girl, remarking that they would not then be tempted to buy inferior oranges at the theater and waste their money. Then he called for a sedan chair and the party set forth for Drury Lane.

During the ride to the theater — which took some time since Mr. Sancho was no light load, and for a girl on each knee the bearers required additional money, another bearer and a stop for refreshments — Mr. Sancho talked. He talked of books — he was a tremendous reader both of novels and of sermons — and he had fully convinced Pansy, if not Jenny, by the time they reached Drury Lane that she must model her style on that of Mr. Sterne, whom he pronounced the finest genius of the age, or indeed of any age. He had modeled his own style on Mr. Sterne's. This was proof enough, Pansy thought. Certainly Mr. Sancho had a noble style.

Drury Lane was all a-glitter. Pansy thought she had never seen such merriment and excitement, so much finery and so much brawling. Linkboys carrying torches darted everywhere, orange-sellers shouted, there were scuffles and greetings, great lords and ladies in satin and powder pressed through the crowd to take their places.

Mr. Sancho bowed and kissed his hand to a large number of these who bowed their greetings in return.

"Like bullrushes in a windstorm," said Jenny, nudging

Pansy. Mr. Sancho kept up a running patter concerning the audience for the benefit of the girls.

"That is my Lord Mansfield: he has the finest library in London. You may curtsy. Observe the stout gentleman — no, not the one in black, the one in snuff-color. He is indifferent to the niceties of dress. That is the famous Dr. Johnson. His friend, the little one, like a terrier dog, is Mr. Boswell. Ah, there is the President of the Royal Academy, Sir Joshua Reynolds. Good evening to you, sir. My young friends are honored in your acquaintance, sir."

"May we eat our oranges, sir?" whispered Jenny.

"Eat them to your heart's content. Everyone eats oranges."

They found their places in the stalls. There was a flourish of trumpets. The stage glowed. It was a wonderfully deep, mysterious stage, lit from behind. Mr. Sancho kindly explained that this was a new way of lighting stages and greatly improved the play.

The three witches opened the play — funny women in blue aprons and shawls, not, as Pansy murmured to Jenny, much like Madam Melanie. After the witches Lady Macbeth appeared, enormous in black velvet, with a little foot-page who held up her train and darted about after the train like a kitten.

"Bill would play that part very well," whispered Jenny loudly. She had to whisper very loudly indeed to make herself heard, for the audience was noisy and barely attended to the play until Mrs. Siddons began to speak. She had a deep, noble voice and when she declaimed many members of the audience, including Mr. Sancho, gave way to tears. Pansy too gave way to tears but for another reason.

She had read *Macbeth* with Mr. Scrooby and to hear it now after so long a time had passed made her homesick. Jenny laughed at the witches and cried bitterly at the death of Lady MacDuff.

The play ended and the audience composed itself to hear the short piece to follow.

"A song," said Mr. Sancho. "We are to hear a song by an Italian gentleman. He has had a tremendous success in the colonies and now performs in England for the first time. He is Signor Antonio. He has performed for sultans and potentates all over the Far East, or so I understand." But Pansy did not hear the end of this sentence, for walking out to the front of the stage, bowing with his arms outstretched in a wide welcoming gesture, was her tutor, Master Anthony.

She could hardly contain her excitement through the song that followed, "Sento nel Cuore," the first song she had learned with him. In the applause that followed she began to shout and gesture to Mr. Sancho, who had some difficulty in understanding that she must immediately join the singer on the stage. When he finally realized who the singer was and what Pansy wanted, however, he was nearly as excited as Pansy. He left his seat and taking the two girls with him he escorted them to the wings where he sent a message to Master Anthony that a friend wished most urgently to see him.

Standing backstage at the theater Pansy waited in wild impatience while actors and actresses swished by her, jostling and laughing. There was a reek of tallow and a heavy smell of powder and pomatum. Once the gorgeous Mrs. Siddons swept by in her velvet which seemed to wish to cling to everything that it touched. And then Master Anthony came blinking off the stage searching through the half-gloom of the greenroom where Pansy and her party waited for the friend whom she so urgently wished to see.

"Sir." she cried, "Master Anthony!"

"Pansy! Pansy Scrooby!" He could hardly believe his eyes and his ears. And he could not even stop that moment to hear how they had found each other because the audience was calling for another song. But he could not bear to part with Pansy and he returned to the stage leading her by the hand, bowing to the ladies and gentlemen and asking leave to introduce his little panther. Then he and Pansy sang together at Drury Lane while the lords and ladies and honest tradesmen and the orange-sellers of London cheered the Italian tenor and the *belle sauvage*. Even Mrs. Siddons was heard to remark that Pansy sang beautifully.

And afterwards as they all drove home in a hired coach to explain matters to Lady Mary and Miss Forsyth, Pansy found leisure to enquire for the tiger.

"He remains with Prudence," said Master Anthony, "the sole reminder of happier times. He eats the bread of adversity."

"We also have eaten a good deal of that bread," remarked Pansy, "but not now. I hope the tiger doesn't mind too much and surely he must be a great comfort to the Scroobys."

"I think it extremely likely," said Master Anthony gravely. "Are you happy, little panther? You look well.

You are finely dressed and are grown tall and handsome. Are your new friends good to you?"

"Oh, very good, sir. But I think all the time on Prudence — and on Squire and Madam. Does Prudence read to Mr. Scrooby? She still couldn't when I went away."

"She reads," said Master Anthony. "But the Scroobys lack you dreadfully. After you went Mistress Prudence was naughtier than ever and the squire

said that nobody would ever read as well and as patiently as you."

"Oh," sighed Pansy. "I must indeed return home. And now I may, may I not? For I have sung at Drury Lane and now I can sing the Scroobys out of adversity."

Miss Forsyth, although much put about by Pansy's disappearance, was too happy to see her back again to do more than scold. And later Captain Forsyth declared the whole episode to have been a blessing in disguise since it had afforded both himself and his aunt such valuable new acquaintances as Master Anthony and Mr. Sancho. Master Anthony became a regular guest at Miss Forsyth's evening parties and sang incessantly to her and her friends, and Mr. Sancho provided them with truffles and hothouse vegetables as well as bombarding them with interesting letters. He was much addicted to letter writing and he wrote to Pansy from time to time in order to help her to form a good, flowing, literary style.

From that time on Pansy's good fortune did nothing but increase. As Captain Forsyth had promised he made her his ward and saw to it that she had the best of masters in all of her studies. He bought her a pony and taught her to cut a good figure on horseback. He commissioned his friend, Sir Joshua Reynolds, to paint her portrait and he introduced her to Mr. Sheridan, who was much captivated by her and her voice. Captain Forsyth also settled a sum of money on her for a dowry.

"It is all very well to gamble, Sophia," he said, "but we may not always hold winning cards. Nor are all players as absentminded as Aunt Forsyth. A little something in the six per cents is worth four aces any day of the week."

But Pansy did not forget the Scroobys. Sometimes she was quite unhappy in all her happiness, thinking of Prudence eating the bread of adversity, and she yearned to find her and bring her to London. Prudence would love London, she thought, and she never wearied of devising schemes to bring her friend across the sea for a season.

At last in the summer of 1782 Captain Forsyth granted her her heart's desire. He arranged for Pansy to make a trip to Canada to find her friends. Before she set sail for North America Captain Forsyth consulted an attorney in order to make certain that Pansy was in no danger of again being taken as a slave. While waiting for the lawyer to give his opinion on the subject of her position Pansy experienced some anxiety.

"It is distressing," she said to Captain Forsyth, "to be constantly wondering who one is and to whom one belongs."

"You belong to the Lord Chancellor," said the captain. "And you are Pansy. Is that not good enough?"

"I am content with Pansy," she replied. "But I am not sure that the Lord Chancellor takes notice of me. One might as well belong to the King.

"Ah, but the Lord Chancellor is only mad north-northwest. The King is mad all around the compass."

When the attorney's answer came back she received quite a shock. "Miss Sophia Scrooby belongs to the King of Spain," he said.

Pansy burst into tears and began to wring her hands.

"Pray do not discommode yourself, miss," said the lawyer, wiping his spectacles. His Majesty will never trouble you. As nearly as I can ascertain Miss Scrooby became, several years ago, through a transaction legal in the United States of America, the property of a certain Pedro Alvarez, a pirate and a subject of the Spanish Crown. According to my latest information this Alvarez was hanged in the year '79 for piracy in Kingstown, Jamaica, all property of his being confiscated to his lawful sovereign. All well and good. Unless of course I am mistaken in the charges which led to the condemnation of the criminal. If it appears that he was hanged for either heresy or blasphemy Miss Scrooby is the property of the Pope of Rome. Since the laws of England do not recognize the right of anyone, even the King of Spain and the Pope, to hold a slave we must conclude that Miss Scrooby in actual fact belongs to herself. However, in the event that any claim of ownership be urged against her upon her visit to the United States, we shall fall back on the Spanish solution as the one most ready to hand. I trust, Miss Scrooby, that you are satisfied. And recollect that after all you are Captain Forsyth's ward."

And so Pansy traveled to the New World under the protection of Master Anthony, who had made an engagement to give a concert in New York. Pansy and the music master set sail from Bristol Harbor on a fine day in July. They reached Halifax three months later when the trees of North America were all on fire from the first frost and from Halifax they started a search for the Scroobys.

The search took some time. In the war years the Scroobys had moved from household to household, going first to their relatives in Canada, but returning before the end of the war to Connecticut, where Madam Scrooby had fallen heiress to a small freehold in the town of

Guilford. As far as her Canadian cousins knew she was living there now. The cousins feared that their circumstances were very much straitened for the war had made everyone poor. So Pansy and Master Anthony, much relieved to have any kind of news, made ready to return to the Republic. They had remained three months in Canada in their fruitless search for the Scroobys and it was now December.

"Do you know, we might come to the Scroobys at Christmas," said Pansy to Master Anthony. "I should like that of all things."

# CHAPTER 18

*Epilogue*
*In which Sophia Scrooby comes home.*

HE WIND was blowing and a light snow was beginning to fall. Prudence Scrooby, her long red hair blowing about her face, was returning from a ramble in the woods beyond the little farmhouse in Guilford, where she had gone to fetch a bough to place across the chimneypiece in honor of Christmas. She had hoped if possible to find some mistletoe, "though whom I should kiss," sighed Prudence, "I surely don't know. But perhaps someone will come."

She found no mistletoe; only bittersweet, but she plucked it and thought she might silver it to look like mistletoe. As she came in sight of the farmhouse she saw that something had disturbed the doves which usually perched upon the ridgepole. Three white birds fluttered over the roof of the little red house and then vanished amid snowflakes into the woods. It was a pretty sight and to Prudence's somewhat discouraged mind a good omen. She went into the house and called to her parents.

"See, I've brought a Christmas bough. I shall gild it and paint the berries silver and we shall celebrate Christmas. What a day it is! It puts me in mind of the day Pansy came — the snow everywhere, and it was just before Christmas I think. Are you ready for me to read, Papa?"

"As you please, Prudence, if your mother does not require you."

"Read to your father, Prudence, do," said Madam Scrooby. "Let me light the candles."

"I hate those candles," said Prudence. "They stink, Mamma. Let me read by the firelight."

"It grows too dark, child. I shall try to get you wax ones for Christmas. But they are so dear. What is it, Mop? Why do you bark? Prudence, I declare, there is someone at the door. It could be Goodwife Holmes come about the butter."

Prudence went to the door and opened it. The snow was blowing harder now and the person she saw on the threshold stood in a flurry of flakes like feathers.

"Prudence!" cried Pansy.

There stood Pansy Scrooby on the threshold, just as she had stood long ago, a slight dark figure with glowing eyes and outstretched hands, taller now of course, but Prudence was taller too. "Oh, Prudence. I have come home."

For a moment Prudence could not speak. Then with a cry she flung her arms about Pansy and began to weep.

"What is it, Prudence?" called Mr. Scrooby from his place by the fire. "Who is there?"

"Oh, Papa, you'll never guess." She took Pansy by the hand and led her to the squire's chair. He was seated there, erect as ever, his blue coat somewhat worn, his linen snowy and his white eyes gazing before him. On the wall behind him was Master Anthony's picture of the family at Scrooby's Acres.

"It is Pansy, sir, Pansy Scrooby come home."

He gave a violent start. "Pansy! Sophia Scrooby! Pre-

served! I can scarcely believe it." He caught her in his arms
and passed his hand over her features as though to make
sure they were really hers. Master Anthony, who had
followed her into the house, began to give him every
assurance that it was really Pansy whom he had brought
home and not some other girl of the same name, and Mop,
older and stouter now but still the same silky and enthusiastic Mop, danced about the family and barked. Madam
Scrooby ran to the kitchen door and called for Master
Anthony's tiger, whom she had gentled into a household
pet, and he came in, arched his back, and spat.

"How happy he is to see me!" cried Master Anthony,

fondling him. "So now you are a free tiger! A revolutionary tiger. Do you still kill chickens?"

And so after many embraces Pansy and Master Anthony sat down by the fire and told all their adventures. Master Anthony would have made it seem that he and Pansy had conquered whole nations and swum oceans to reach the Scroobys but Pansy tried to stick to the plain facts.

"Oh, Pansy, you sound as though you had lived in the Arabian Nights all of these years," sighed Prudence. "How I envy you! Only fancy, Drury Lane! But I did learn to read, Pansy. Did you read to the great folk in London?"

"Nay," said Pansy. "They had no taste for reading. I sang to them and played cards with them."

"Oh, Pansy, I know it is wicked to be covetous but I should dearly love to go to a London rout — and dance and gamble."

"That you shall, Prudence. We shall go to Ranelagh together one day and play cards and dance and make riddles. I learned to make riddles in London and it is better sport than cards. And Mr. Sancho taught me a literary style."

Here Mr. Scrooby expressed a strong wish that Pansy should sing for him and so Master Anthony struck up a tune. They sang "Sento nel Cuore" and then "To Anacreon in Heaven," which Madam Scrooby declared was loud enough and fine enough to awaken the whole Republic. And after the music was done they sat down to a feast which Pansy and Master Anthony had brought — two fowls and a bottle of wine. They sat long over the meal while the Scroobys recounted their wanderings and lamented how sadly Prudence's education had been neglected since Pansy left.

After supper they played at riddles. The older Scroobys had once or twice played at riddles in their younger days but Prudence had never done it and pronounced the game a dreadful mental strain. She could not be persuaded to get beyond "My first." Madam Scrooby also complained that she could not get the words to fit the rhymes or the meaning to fit the words but Mr. Scrooby had no difficulty at all and presented the following riddle to Pansy, since he had no other Christmas gift for her:

> *My first a gem, brought from the ocean's deeps*
> *Where ancient Triton his cold council keeps.*
> *My second is the dawn with rosy fingers,*
> *Who in the morning clouds serenely lingers.*
> *My third's the darkness which o'erspreads the sky*
> *Until my second's chariot draws night.*
> *My third being fled, my fourth appears to crown*
> *The day with light and shine his splendor down*
> *Upon my fifth, which is that happy time*
> *When life is sweet and strength is in the prime.*
> *And for my whole: a certain garden flower*
> *Heartsease, that blooms in sunshine and in shower.*

Prudence later worked the riddle into a sampler, a bunch of pansies on a blue background with the riddle embroidered underneath together with the date of Pansy's return to the Scroobys.

It was midnight before they had finished wth their stories and their games. Prudence pulled the window curtains aside and stood with Master Anthony's tiger in her arms, gazing at the morning star which hung in the cold winter sky like a beacon above the white landscape. The snow lay along the orchard boughs like flowers. Mr. Scrooby called the family to prayers and when these had been said Pansy sang one last song to welcome in the holiday, "Lo, How a Rose E'er Blooming," while the snows of Christ's Nativity drifted softly over the fields and woods and pastures of New England.